Pudding, Poison & Pie

by

Sigrid Vansandt

ISBN-13: 978-1523294299

D1490684

Pudding, Poison & Pie

CHAPTER 1

"It will have blood they say; blood will have blood."

-William Shakespeare, MacBeth, Act III, Scene IV

Marsden-Lacey, England

Present Day

Amos, the pint-sized maltipoo, curled up warm next to Martha as a mournful, winter wind howled outside Flower Pot Cottage. A storm was winding its way down from the high hills of the Yorkshire Dales and into the sleeping village of Marsden-Lacey. Soft snow fell, leaving a thick, white blanket of the cold stuff on roof tops, gardens and quiet, empty streets. No living thing stirred the nighttime peace. Cozily tucked between a feather bed and two heavy quilts, Martha Littleword drifted off to sleep.

"The world is ending next week," the dark-haired woman whispered into Martha's ear. Martha pulled back and laughed as if in reaction to a shared joke, but the woman's face betrayed no emotion as she turned and left the room. As Martha watched, she became smaller, the intense light from the hallway blotting out

the edges of her silhouette and blurring the remainder of her retreating figure.

"I don't believe you!" Martha called to the departing prophet of doom as she was swallowed up by the darkness. "You're just saying that to make me follow you. I won't! I won't do it!"

Martha stood firm, and instead of pursuing the woman, she wrapped the red blanket from the couch around her. Its warmth comforted her and helped to block the intense cold of the room.

Where was Merriam? He'd promised to be here. He had lied. I can't do it anymore, she thought. I wish Helen would come home. It's too lonely here.

Sounds coming from the kitchen caught her attention. Cabinet doors slamming caused a seed of panic to take root in her stomach. Metal on metal, like the sharpening of a blade, came from somewhere inside the house. A cold feeling of fear crawled up Martha's spine. The hair on her skin raised in warning as the room became colder causing her breath to hang in white wisps.

Instinct told her to run, but she couldn't move. Muscle numbing horror riveted her to the spot. The earlier bright light emanating from the hall was gone, replaced by a brooding darkness, pulsating with evil and cruelty. She silently screamed instructions to her body to listen and to move. She needed to get out of the house. Finally, her body found its will and she ran to the front door, slinging it open just as a hand clamped down on her shoulder. An excruciating pain dug into her back.

Whirling around, she saw her attacker's face contorted with a twisted joy. A sharp pain stabbed her abdomen, causing her to lean forward. With her last bit of strength, Martha gave the female attacker a great shove, hoping to push her back into the black gulf of hell from whence she'd sprung. The force of the blow caused the woman's knife to fall from her hand, striking a knothole and lodging blade-up in the floor. Off balance, she seemed to fall in slow motion, her facial expression one of shock and surprise.

The sound of the body hitting the ground and a hellish scream made Martha recoil from the sickening sight. The woman lay on her back, skewered by her own knife. Blood began to spread. She writhed and grabbed for Martha, her hands like claws, her face almost preternaturally cruel. With the life streaming out of the woman on the floor, Martha dropped to her knees. She clasped both hands together in a gesture of prayer over the dying woman, who now lay lifeless and still.

"No!" she cried. "I didn't mean to!"

Martha's brain climbed upward, through the fog of fear and repulsion, forcing her consciousness to swim along with it. Her muscles found their power for action, bringing her upright into a sitting position. Clammy and with blurry eyes, she tried desperately to find a focal point in the dark room.

Her gaze locked onto the steady, gentle light coming from the street lamp outside her bedroom window. She didn't dare shut her eyes but kept them riveted to the light. Soon, her shaking subsided and Martha realized she was, mercifully, at last, awake.

CHAPTER 2

Stratford, England

1623

Judith stirred the contents of a large copper saucepan. The August heat in the kitchen was stifling. She'd spent the morning preparing a chicken broth for her mother, Anne, who'd been ill.

Both of Judith's boys were playing somewhere out in the large farm yard and she hoped they would stay quietly out of trouble until she finished her task. Anne told Judith not to worry about her and to let Mitty, the cook, prepare the meal, but Judith wanted to do it. Anne and Judith shared a deeper understanding than most mothers and daughters. They'd both lost young children to the plague. Anne had always been there for her children and the preparation of the rich broth was a loving act by a devoted daughter.

Judith climbed the back stairs of the large, rambling house her mother called home. The house's name was New Place. William, Judith's father, bought it for his family once his fortune was secure. It would never be Judith's home again. The entire estate would go to her older sister, Susanna, but Judith never expected it anyway. She'd realized early on what really mattered was not the gift of things, but the gift of human love.

That didn't mean, though, that she wasn't pragmatic. Today was more exhausting than usual for Judith. Her children were at the age where they were exceptionally needy, money was always tight and the care of her sick mother over the last few weeks was wearing Judith down, both physically and mentally.

Reaching the top of the stairs and the door to her mother's bedchamber, she tapped gently. "Mother? I've brought you something to eat," she said softly, not wanting to startle Anne.

Pushing the door open, she bent her neck around to see if the invalid was sleeping. In a massive four-poster bed, propped up on a hefty pile of feather pillows, slept her Anne. Judith saw the shallow rise and fall of her mother's chest, which relieved the younger woman greatly. In the last few days, she'd become increasingly concerned that, at some point, she would walk in and find her best friend asleep forever.

The older mother's eyes flickered open and a soft smile creased the aged and weathered face, testifying to her long association with life's joys and worry's.

"Is that you, my darling?" her mother asked.

"Yes, dear. Are you hungry?"

The still bright eyes looked up at the warm summer light filtering hazily through the clear glass window panes. There was a mellowness to Anne's unhurried response.

"No. I'm no longer hungry," she said with a quiet smile.

Judith cocked her head to one side. She knew her mother meant more by the simple statement, but she wasn't ready to let the only person who ever truly loved her, understood her, and fought for her, leave this life yet. It was too much too soon.

The old mother, being wise about the needs of children, knew this, too, so she took the broth being proffered by her youngest of three and with benign resignation drank her soup dutifully.

After Anne had put the bowl down to rest upon her lap, she summoned the energy to ask her daughter a question.

"Do you know if your father's things are ready for Mr. Condell? He was supposed to come by this week."

"Yes, everything he asked for is ready. All of Father's foul copies left in his desk are in a case for him."

"Good. Those are the last of his first draft copies he used in the theatre. Mr. Condell and Mr. Hemmings have put such effort toward this folio."

Anne shut her eyes, as if exhausted by the effort to eat and talk. Soon, she slept. Taking the bowl and opening one of the hinged windows to allow fresh air to enter the room, Judith let herself out, her mind on the many tasks still ahead of her.

Anne Hathaway Shakespeare, Judith's mother, died four days later. Because Shakespeare's daughters were illiterate, they weren't able to write Anne's epitaph, but with the help of

Susanna's husband, they composed a beautiful remembrance in honor of her. They laid Anne to rest next to her famous husband and their father, William.

It is worth noting that Anne was never known to have traveled from Stratford, to have been able to read or write, or to have lived a life beyond the simple one of a wife and mother. What is curious about her is that though her husband's legacy is one beyond measure to the world, so might hers have been, as well, due to the great love her children certainly felt for her. The great bard's epitaph is written in stone; Anne's is not. Hers is written upon a brass plate, not a cheap material during the seventeenth century and much more valuable than stone.

Brass would be immortal, and this may have been what Anne's children wished most for their beloved mother.

The words on her grave were:

"Thou, my mother, gave me life, and thy breast, milk. Alas ! For such great bounty to me, I shall give thee a tomb. How much rather I would entreat the good angel to move the stone, so that thy figure might come forth, as did the body of Christ; but my prayers avail nothing. Come quickly, O Christ; so that my mother, closed in the tomb, may rise again and seek the stars."

When you consider Judith and Susanna were uneducated and not given the opportunity to write their famous father's epitaph, they succeeded beautifully when it came to their mother's. Anne's legacy was one of great love and sacrifice. Some might say the most eternal gift of all.

CHAPTER 3

Marsden-Lacey, England

Present Day

"You need a rest," Helen Ryes, an extremely well-dressed, pretty, brunette of about forty or so years of age was saying to her friend, Martha, a curvaceous redhead who, at the moment, was feeling whiny.

Martha Littleword gingerly put her teacup down into its saucer and slumped in the tall, chintz-covered wingback chair. She'd been working double duty while Helen, her business partner, was out of town for two weeks in New York, seeing a possible client about work to be done on a collection of Audubon prints.

"Would you mind if I went on a little holiday?" Martha asked. "Maybe a long weekend somewhere quiet with a spa. I want a massage every day, cheese plates without fruit, and a wonderfully soft bed with too many fluffy pillows."

Martha put two teaspoons of sugar in her tea and reached for a lemony-looking poppyseed muffin sitting daintily on the two-tiered china plate. The two friends were catching up at Marsden-Lacey's best teashop, Harriet's.

Helen reached across the lace tablecloth and patted Martha's hand solicitously.

"You deserve it, and I think the business should pay for it," she offered with a mischievous twinkle in her eye. "The business is doing so well, and our list of clients is growing. Mr. Fukushima emailed me that he likes our bid. It looks like we'll be going back to New York in March.

Martha's eyes narrowed. She'd come to recognize a certain tone in Helen's voice. It reeked of something, as yet, unannounced.

"Go ahead, tell me what's up," Martha said."Well…I've heard from Lord Percy Farthingay's heir, a Mr. Brickstone, in Warwickshire. It's only about two hours from here. He wants us to come down to look at an unusual manuscript he's unearthed in his uncle's library."

"And…" Martha said in a coaxing way sure to encourage Helen to completely spill the beans.

Becoming more animated than her usual prim manner, Helen gushed, "Oh, Martha! It may be an old prompt from The Globe Theatre in London. Not just any prompt, either, one from when William Shakespeare and his collaborator, John Fletcher were writing for the King's Men."

"Uh, huh," Martha said, without much enthusiasm. "And, so that I get this right, you think we should go *together* to meet Lord Feathergay…"

"Lord Farthingay," Helen corrected, beginning to pull out a compact mirror from her purse. She discreetly checked her smile for spinach.

"Farthingay, so sorry," Martha acquiesced in a bored tone. "He needs both of us on this jaunt to Warwickshire?"

"No, probably not, but I'd love to have you with me. I miss my buddy. Besides, you could snuggle up in a nice estate hotel while I talk to Feathergay. I mean FARTHINGAY!"

They both giggled.

The girls were enjoying a new lease on mid-life. After Helen's husband, George, ran off with his nubile, twenty-something assistant, Helen had been in need of help in a bad way. The works-on-paper restoration business she and George owned was impossible for one person to run alone. Martha, on the other hand, was suffering from empty-nest syndrome, a dull existence at home, and a boring job as a paralegal.

Kismet or karma, depending on how you looked at it, had landed both of them in the middle of a local murder investigation. The two new friends hit it off and decided to solve the murder. Once they survived that adventure, they decided to work together in Helen's business.

These days, the new endeavor was going smashingly well. Since they'd teamed up, they'd managed to survive two raving lunatics, and save five treasures lost to time; the working arrangement played to both their strengths.

"You haven't been home for even two days. Don't you want to see Piers before we head off to Warwickshire?" Martha asked, trying to entice Helen to stay put by other means. If she had to use Piers Cousins, an attractive ex-client of theirs who had sparked-up a flirtation with Helen, as the bait to slow Helen down, then so be it.

"He's not here. He's in London. I thought..." Helen hesitated to finish.

"What?"

"He might join us."

"Good. I'll be left to my own devices: sleeping, sleeping some more, and lounging."

"You're incorrigible," Helen said and then laughed.

"I'm pooped," Martha retorted and popped the last bite of the poppyseed muffin into her mouth.

"When is Kate coming home from university for Christmas?" Helen asked.

"In about a week and a half. She's bringing a *friend*." Martha's eyebrows danced up and down twice. "Any advice?"

Helen put the mirror back in her purse in a deliberate manner, picked up her teacup, and stared off through the curtained window at the falling snow.

"I remember the first time my Christine brought home a *friend*." Helen chuckled lightly. "He barely topped the scales at a hundred and twenty pounds and had long hair tied up in some kind of weird-looking bun on his head. For two days, he followed me around the house telling me about his body-building routine."

Helen rolled her eyes and turned to look at Martha directly.

"What a dud, but fortunately at the time, Christine had attention deficit when it came to men, and he was quickly replaced by a new love d'jour in a few short weeks. The short answer to your question is, if you don't like him, keep quiet and pray for the best."

Martha nodded.

"That's good advice. She's been so secretive about her boyfriends, so for her to bring one home may mean it's serious."

"Maybe, but he's not your boyfriend; he's hers. She's your daughter, so she must have a good head on her shoulders."

Martha sat back in her chair and gave Helen a grateful smile.

"Ahhh, thank you. I knew there was a reason I kept you around."

She put her napkin on the table.

"I think we'd better get back to theFlower Pot. Amos, Gus, and Vera are probably in need of a stretch. They've been hugging the fireplace since the last snow."

The girls stood up after waving goodbye to Harriet. Grabbing their hats, coats, mufflers, and gloves to ward off the outside cold, they pulled open the door and pushed through the low-beamed aperture, into a winter wonderland, Yorkshire style.

Having snowed on and off for three days, the weather was perfect for this time of year. Everywhere you looked, rounded mounds of the white stuff clung to thatched roofs, tucked up against hedgerows, and covered the ground in pillowy softness. The villagers were in the throes of seasonal decorating. Traditional mixtures of conifers, rosemary, holly berries and pine cones were stuffed into woven willow branches to create swags and wreaths. The cheerful foliage bedecked doors and windows along streets and alleyways making the entire village a lovely Christmas present waiting for good Saint Nicholas to arrive.

"I love England at Christmas," Martha said as they walked down one of the alleys. "It looks like an illustration from a children's book. Do you remember 'Wind in the Willows'?"

"I do," Helen replied.

"Remember the picture where Mole and Rat are wandering through the wintery medieval village lane? They're looking in the cozy, warm windows and you wished as a child you lived there," Martha said.

"Yes, that's it exactly," Helen agreed. "I wanted to live in Badger's Hole, eat at his table, sleep in the comfy beds and warm myself by the fire."

The two friends were quiet for a while ruminating on memories from childhood and how nostalgia goes part and parcel with the Christmas season. As they made their way along High Street looking in the shop windows, they resembled the two childhood characters they'd been discussing. One pointed out a pretty scarf and one noted the dog coats for sale in Mr. Poindexter's store.

"Are you going home, Helen, to be with your children this year?" Martha asked. "You know how much Kate and I would love to have you with us."

"Oh, I know, and thank you for the offer, but I'm going to spend it with my son, Timothy, and his family. The rest of my kids come to Concord the following week."

"You're hopping the big pond a lot lately," Martha said, giving Helen a playful nudge in the side.

"Haven't I, though? Some days I wonder if it would be easier to move over there."

Martha didn't say anything. A sudden lump rose up in her throat. After a pause, she said, "Well, it would stink if you left, but I've always been a big believer that family always comes first."

"Don't be trying to get rid of me yet," Helen responded with a laugh. "I love my home here, my friends and the jury is still out on Mr. Cousins."

Martha teased Helen a bit. "Well, you'd better snag him soon, Helen, because the word on the street is Lovely Lana is back in town."

"What?" Helen stopped dead in the middle of the cobblestone sidewalk. "Lana's back in Marsden-Lacey?" she squeaked, her arms hanging limply on each side.

Martha hadn't realized how well the mark would hit when she'd fired it off, but she played it for all it was worth.

"Yep, I talked with Celine Rupert yesterday. She said Lana was at Healy to visit everyone."

Helen threw her hands up in frustration. "I leave this village for one week, one freaking week, and Lana from Louisiana, rolls back into town. She's a judge for the Bake-Off?"

"Yep, she is. I'm telling you, Helen, that dream of mine must have been prophetic. Something is in the air: Merriam is acting weird. Lana's in town. And you have us running off to Warwickshire to meet," Martha said with deliberate rottenness, "old Feathergay."

"Farthingay!" Helen practically shouted with irritation.

"Oh, yeah, Fartingay," Martha said, but unable to hold it in any longer, she burst out laughing.

"Farthingay! Farthingay!" Helen stamped her foot in irritation.

"I'm messing with you, H. I like to see you get all riled up. It's bad of me, I know, but you never disappoint."

Martha turned to walk away.

Out of nowhere, a huge clump of snow splattered against Martha's head, stopping her chuckling and completely arresting her feet.

"Why you little…" she said, turning around only to receive another icy blast of the wet stuff directly in her face.

Helen doubled over in an all-out laughing fit. "I can't move," she said, holding herself. "You so deserved that!" she cried.

"You'd better high-tail it home, Ryes, because you've taken on the best snowball fighter the South ever saw," Martha said, bending down to scoop up her retaliatory snow missile.

"The South? Ha!" Helen called, her position uphill from Martha on the quiet lane. The street lamps flickered into life, giving a soft glow to the newly fallen snow. "It hardly ever snows south of the Mason-Dixon Line, so quit talking and let's see what you're made of."

A wicked smile stretched across Martha's face, but froze instantly as another ball of snow whacked her from behind. She spun around to see only the brim of a hat quickly dart back behind the edge of a stone house. Whoever threw the snowball was short.

"Who's there?" she called good-humoredly. A child's face peeked around the corner. The owner was smiling broadly and Martha realized it was Piers' young adopted son, Emerson.

"Helen, look who's here. It's Emmy! Come on out, Emmy. I call a truce until we get to say a proper hello."

Emerson poked his head out and gave the girls a good assessment. Boys know instinctively that people participating in a snowball fight are rarely trustworthy.

"Hello, Mrs. Ryes and Mrs. Littleword," he said still hugging the safety of the house's protective shield.

"Ahh, come on over, Emmy. We promise to be ladies. It's a firm truce," Martha said.

"Keep an eye on them, Emerson, particularly that redhead. She always has an ulterior motive."

Detective Chief Inspector Merriam Johns leaned around the corner of the same house Emerson had stepped out away from only seconds earlier. The Chief's eyes twinkled with humor and a challenge.

"That's a terrible thing to teach a child, Chief Johns," Martha countered. "Who left this young mind in your jaded hands?"

Johns patted the top of Emerson's head. "Emmy and I were on our way to the Village Hall to see how the preparations are going for the Pudding and Pie Bake-Off. He's helping me while his nanny finishes up. She's in the competition, too."

Helen came up to stand beside Martha. The wind was picking up with the setting of the sun, making the three adults shiver.

"Would you like to come to my cottage first, Emerson? I made peanut butter chocolate chip cookies yesterday and I have some beef stew. This gruff old hound dog you're running with probably hasn't even thought to offer you food."

Martha bent down to the boy's level. She loved children and always knew when they needed something.

"May we, Chief Johns?" Emerson asked, excited by the chance at a sweet treat.

"Hound dog? I'll have you know, Mrs. Littleword," Johns countered, "that I intended to feed the boy. They've got left over meat pies tonight at The Traveler's."

Everyone knew the Chief was good at sussing out free food. He had to be. Polly, his mother, was usually too busy with her brewing business and he, himself, didn't have time due to his work schedule.

During his rounds each week, he received many gratuitous treats. A fresh piece of pie at Harriet's, a taste of the local pub's new menu offerings, or the multitude of teas with dainty sandwiches, cheese quiches and homemade biscuits made by the older ladies of Marsden-Lacey were constantly being offered to the Constabulary's top man.

Martha shook her head and gave Johns a woeful look. "Well, I'm offering real food and a yummy after-dinner dessert. Emmy wants to try my cookies, and you're welcome to come, too, Panhandle. There's plenty, but I've got to get going. Gus, Vera and Amos need their dinner and a stretch in the garden."

"Come on and go with us, Chief," Helen said. "Martha's a pretty good cook herself. She could give the Pudding and Pie competitors a run for their money."

Johns never passed up a free meal, so the four friends headed off to Flower Pot Cottage where a warm fire, good food, and three furry greeters waited hopefully for the return of their favorite person.

CHAPTER 4

London, 1634

The cat lazily sunned herself in a puddle of summer sunlight. Bees hummed in the drowsy heat while gathering their pollen among the rich array of hollyhocks, roses, daffodils, and tall, white daisies. The garden was a wonderful place for a mature cat to while away the hours cleaning her coat or waiting for a hapless bird to flit too closely to one of her many hiding spots. She no longer had the agility to actually catch one, but a nice chase was good for the soul and justified a long nap later.

She'd been able to come and go between the house and the garden at her convenience most of her life. Her favorite place was upstairs in the deep chair belonging to the person she attended. They'd spent many long hours together. He called her Minerva in a playful way because of her cat-like wisdom. It was a name they both agreed upon.

Lately, with him gone, she'd spent more time outside in this well-tended kingdom of her own. As a cat, she wasn't privy to the reasons people came and went, but she knew Death when it arrived, and it visited the house only last week. Minerva lost her human of many years. The others called him Edward and it was lonely for her since his death.

With feline grace, the grey tabby lifted herself onto all four of her dainty paws. She sat for a few moments blinking her beautiful green eyes and then closing them against the glare of the July sun. The tinkling of the house's front bell rang, catching her attention. Minerva, unlike some of her sisters, was a social cat when it came to visitors. She made haste toward the entryway, subtly trotting close to the wall as to avoid any of the servants who might trip over her.

A tall, thin man waited patiently there on a bench by the door. He was a stranger to her, but never-the-less, she gave him her standard Blount House welcome that she, as its mascot, always confirmed upon its guests.

A slow approach is best, as any cat knows, to give the human a chance to become aware of its presence. The next step is a nice mew of 'hello' and, if all goes well, a hospitable feline will perform a rub with her tail held high. Minerva advanced.

"Good morning," the man said with warmth and appreciation. He bent down and stroked the silky fur while the grey feline purred appreciatively.

"You are a beauty, my sweet one. Would you let me hold you?" the man asked.

Minerva sat regally beside his leg, two front paws neatly placed together slightly touching, while her tail wrapped protectively around them. She waited until she was certain of the goodness of his aura and gently jumped up into his waiting lap.

"I had a cat once when I was a boy," he murmured lovingly. "She lives with my mother in Warwickshire."

Minerva relaxed under his gentle scratches and light petting.

Soon, a plump woman with an apron covered in flour, sauntered down the long, low hall. It was the cook, Saphy, and no one, not even Minerva, impeded her daily routine.

"My mistress is not at home. She's left London because of the plague. What is your business?" she asked brusquely of the young man who shifted his gaze back and forth between Saphy and the cat.

"My name is Harry Dudens. Master Blount and I worked together. He asked that I bring certain documents, plays actually, back to Mistress Shakespeare. They were ones she loaned to him through Mr. Heminges and Mr. Condell. I spoke with Mistress Blount about it last week."

Saphy indicated by a wave of her hand, that he should come with her into another room off the hall.

"The papers my mistress left for you are tied up in a bundle. Let me find them. They should have a red ribbon..." On the table sat stacks of documents of every order imaginable. Books lined the bookshelves and the young man took a quick opportunity to read the titles. Marlow's *Hero and Leander,* Shelton's translation of *Don Quixote,* and *Mr. William Shakespeare's Comedies,*

Histories and Tragedies sat side by side with other works known to have been published by the Edward Blount's Black Bear Booksellers in St. Paul's Churchyard.

"These must be what you came for," Saphy said, holding out to him a dusty pile of manuscripts. The man reached across the bureau and took the heavy load of papers from the cook. He glanced down at the top of the bundle, noting the first play. It was called *Cardenna*. Not recognizing it as one of Shakespeare's, he quickly thumbed through the rest. Seeing *The Tempest* and *Measure for Measure*, he knew this was the right group.

They showed signs of age and human handling. Stains from smeared ink blots, ash, and, perhaps, even food and drink were there for anyone to trace the manuscripts' interaction with humans.

"Thank you, madam. Please tell your lady thank you, as well," Harry said. "Do you expect her back soon? I would like to talk to her about the other books in the library."

"Oh, I doubt she will return. The plague is so terrible this time and having lost her husband and with little money to live on, she's released most of us. I'm the only servant she's offered a place at her sister's home."

Harry looked down at the cat sitting so quietly beside his foot.

"Are you taking the cat with you to the country?"

Saphy gave the cat a guilty look, followed by a resigned one. "No, but maybe the auctioneers can find her a home."

"Consider it done," Harry said. He knelt down to the cat and explained her options. Not being a foolish animal, she followed him complacently from Blount House and into the busy street. He picked her up and together they disappeared into the throngs of London's humanity. Minerva never looked back. Cats are survivors and not known for sentimentality.

Two days later, Minerva and Harry were traveling through Warwickshire when they stopped along the way to have a bite to eat in a pub. Not accustomed to trotting long distances, Minerva was carried most of the trip comfortably in Harry's pack. He put her down saying not to wander far and that he was meeting a man inside.

The busy pub was filled with people from all walks of life. Harry found a table and waited. In a short time, a well-dressed gentleman threaded his way through the crowd of patrons and sat down on a stool across from Harry.

"Harry Dudens?" he asked without ceremony.

Harry nodded. "Master Allen?" he asked.

"Yes," the man replied, and, obviously, not wishing to stop long at this local watering hole, he got on with his business.

"Do you have Shakespeare's foul copies?"

Harry pulled out the entire set of plays he'd picked up only two days earlier from Blount's home and handed them over to the man sitting across from him. Master Allen took his time looking over the documents and appearing satisfied that they were indeed what he wanted, he said, "I'll take all five of these. In turn, I'll pay you the agreed upon price. Each play will be copied. The copies will be given to Shakespeare's heirs. Do we have an understanding?"

Harry nodded his agreement. Allen took out a leather pouch handing the entire thing to Harry. Standing up, he walked out.

Being an intelligent young man, Harry didn't count his new found wealth in public. Instead, he wrapped what was left of his fish in some old paper and paid for his meal. With the purse tucked in his breast pocket, he went outside to collect Minerva.

"I've got you a nice bit of fish, my girl."

He scooped her up and stuck her in his knapsack.

By the end of that year, Harry owned a small shop selling books in Skipton, Warwickshire, while Minerva spent her days sunning herself in their back garden.

As for Master Allen, he kept the original foul copies he purchased from Harry that day in the pub. Later, he sold fresh copies to willing buyers. The plays went on to become famous, and the copies he made found their way into other theatre troupe's repertoires fueling the world's interest and love for Shakespeare.

Those fresh copies he produced would be burned in various fires throughout history and some were simply tossed out as unimportant documents. Not so, for Allen's originals. They became buried within his ponderous collection, sleeping unmolested for centuries and accumulating dust until the time they would be found.

CHAPTER 5

Marsden-Lacey, England

Present Day

Snow covered and freezing, Helen, Martha, Chief Johns and Emerson maneuvered through Flower Pot Cottage's front door. Everyone was so encumbered with coats, scarfs, and wellies that it took some time for all the excitement to die down. Martha's menagerie of pets, Amos, a Maltipoo of about five pounds, and Vera and Gus, the two resident cats, greeted everyone.

As people came through the door, three furry four-footers hustled past them to take care of their own business. Helen started the kettle while Johns got to work building up the fire. Emerson followed Martha around the kitchen and answered the bark that announced the pets were ready for re-admittance into the warmth of the house.

"Come and sit by me, Emerson," Martha encouraged the child. She put down a mountainous pile of cookies arranged on a plate, and Helen brought in a tray of cups.

"I've got a treat for you, Emerson," Helen said, with a smile. "My children used to love hot chocolate. Do you?"

"Oh, yes! Senior Agosto makes it for me, but only if it's been a particularly rough day."

"Well, today, it's a treat because we don't get to see you much. Sound good?" Helen asked.

With a cookie already being chewed upon, Emerson's good manners wouldn't allow for a verbal response only a vigorous nod making his blonde curls bounce upon his head.

"Chief, which would you prefer, hot chocolate or tea?" Helen asked, while putting a tea bag in her own cup.

Martha came trotting back into the room. She'd put the stew on to warm.

"I'd love to try the chocolate, Helen. It's been ages since I've had it," Chief Johns said, reaching for a cookie.

"It might be a bit too sweet, Chief. You know us American's, we like our sugar."

She handed him the cup and stood ready with the whipped cream.

"Want some?"

The Chief nodded with enthusiasm much like Emerson before him, and with the blood beginning to circulate better and fingers starting to thaw from holding warm cups, the conversation turned to the Marsden-Lacey First Annual Pudding and Pie Bake-Off.

"What does the competition support?" Martha asked.

"The proceeds are for sending our secondary school's student choir to Disneyland Paris for a choral competition. I've signed up, along with three of my constables, to participate as a team and Emerson's nanny, Miss Rupert is also on a team."

"Helen, we should take part," Martha said excitedly. "How many people to a team?"

"Four, and I know someone who is looking for two more volunteers."

"Who?" Martha asked.

"Mum and her boyfriend, Mr. O'Grady."

Johns didn't look thrilled, but he continued, "They're a handful and Mum is terribly bossy. Somehow, that poor old Grady puts up with it and keeps coming around. Man must be a masochist."

"Let's do it, Helen. I've cooked with Polly before, and it was a great time."

"You both were three sheets to the wind last time," Helen said primly. "Anyone would have fun the way you both cook."

Martha leaned back in the sofa with a feisty look in her eyes and sipped her hot chocolate with massive amounts of whipped cream projecting from the brim. "It was a good time," she said putting emphasis on the word good. "We may have to put Polly on wine restriction, if we plan to win, though."

"For the love of Pete, woman!" Johns said, practically choking on his chocolate. "My mother isn't a drinker. She's never been drunk in her life. If anything, it's your nutter influence that drove her to drink."

Martha shook her head ever so slightly and grinned.

"Nice try, Chief, but she bought the wine and filled my glass, not the other way around."

Helen chuckled under her breath.

"You're starting trouble, Littleword. Stop antagonizing Merriam. You should tell him about your dream instead of casting aspersions on his mother."

Giving Martha a sour look, Johns said, "So you know, those cookies of yours are a bit hard. I've had better from the O'Grady Grocery's half-price bin."

Martha, enjoying the teasing, turned on him and punched him gently on the shoulder. "Then you'd better take the ones you stuffed in your pockets out. I wouldn't want you upsetting your digestion with my day-old cookies."

"Oh, I wasn't going to eat these. I'm going skeet shooting next week with Piers, and I thought these would be fun to use instead."

Martha's red hair took on a life of its own. When her energy flared to a certain heat, the hair lifted as well. Wisps would begin to spring free from the unkempt bun. They danced and bobbed as they caught flight on delicate air currents around her head. She'd always enjoyed a good sparring match, and Johns was equal to the task.

Trying to act highly offended for a good show, Martha turned her attention to Helen.

"I know we have to go to Warwickshire, but the competition starts next Thursday. That gives us four days to come up with our recipes and decide who's making what. Come on, Helen. I know it'll be fun and now I have a reason to make a dish of crow."

"Crow?" Johns said, befuddled.

"Yes, so you can eat it," Martha retorted.

Johns laughed and reached over to give her a peace offering of a kiss on the cheek, but Martha wouldn't have any of it. They'd been seeing each other for two months and things were going extremely well. Martha was happy and enjoying the time they spent together.

"You are on restriction, Chief Johns," she announced. "The gauntlet has been thrown down and I," she flamboyantly bent down to pick up one of John's gloves lying on the coffee table, "am accepting your challenge. Helen, wilt thou be my teammate, or must I look elsewhere for a noble heart?"

"We're learning about Shakespeare's plays in school, Mrs. Ryes," Emerson said, getting in on the conversation. "Mrs. Littlewood is being what my teacher calls theatrical."

"Mrs. Littleword certainly knows how to put on a good show," Helen said. "And to answer your question, Goodwife

Littleword, I give my pledge to do us honor at the Pudding and Pie Bake-off." She good-humoredly gave Chief Johns a steely look. "As for you, Sheriff, be certain of one thing: Southern women know how to throw down in the kitchen."

"Mrs. Ryes!" Martha burst out laughing. "What language! You brought back more than a client from New York."

"What does throw-down mean?" Emerson immediately asked.

"To throw down means to fight or to get extremely serious about something," Helen explained in her best pedagogical tone.

"Whoa, I'm so scared," Johns said in a bored way, with his eyebrows arched for sarcastic effect.

"It's on!" Martha declared and went over to embrace Helen. "Emerson, we must get busy. Want to help me brush up on my tarts?"

But before he could answer, Johns' phone beeped. It was a text message. "Looks like we need to get going in about thirty minutes, Emerson. Miss Rupert says she'll be done in an hour." Then in a mock whisper, "If you do come back to help Mrs. Littleword, make sure you stick some of those tarts in your knapsack. We can use them for door stops at the police station."

A pillow bounced up against Johns' head, making Emerson break out in a giggle. Johns winked at Martha playfully and pushed his luck a bit.

"Is that stew ready? It smells good."

"I'm going to feed Emerson, but you'll be tossed out on your backside, Panhandle, if you say one more thing out of turn about my cooking," Martha said, poking the Chief in his middle.

"I promise to be a most appreciative guest, scout's honor." Johns held three fingers up in the Boy Scout sign as an indication of his better merit.

Everyone settled down around the cozy kitchen table and enjoyed a hearty meal. Amos, the dog, wandered around at everyone's feet and scored an entire piece of stew beef from Emerson, who used a clever coughing trick, to allow him to deftly slip the treat to the waiting furry con beneath the table.

Dinner over, Martha saw the two guests out. Emerson ran ahead to throw himself down on the ground to make a snow angel as Johns turned to Martha and said in a soft voice, "Would you like to come to mum's tomorrow night and ask her about the competition? She's working on a pudding, and there'll be lots of extra for dinner. You can tell me about your dream."

Martha reached over and gave the big, burly man a tight hug. "I like you, you old lug." She held him for a second, thinking back on the dream. A slight shiver ran through her frame.

"You better get inside. It's too cold out here for you," he said lovingly.

Martha smiled up at him. It wasn't the cold making her shiver. She reached up and gave him a quick peck on the mouth. "That'll keep you warm until you get home," she said softly.

He squeezed her goodbye and called to Emerson. "Come along, Emerson. It's time to go."

The two gentlemen waved from the street. Martha shut the door, but not before she saw Mrs. Cuttlebirt, her ever-vigilant neighbor pull back quickly from her window and begin to lower the shade.

Martha couldn't resist teasing her. "Hi, Mrs. Cuttlebirt!" she called loudly and waved in an exaggerated way. "Having a busy evening?"

The window shade flapped back up and the small but plump body wrapped in a flannel housecoat leaned out of the open window. "Doing well, Mrs. Littleword. I see the police chief is calling on you again this evening!"

Martha smiled inwardly. "Oh, yes! He's been over to challenge Helen and me to participate in the Bake-Off. Must be community-minded!"

Mrs. Cuttlebirt nodded appreciatively and backed up into her warm room. "Must be going. It's too cold tonight to hang outside this window for long."

Martha waved and closed her front door, leaning against its solidness. "I wonder what she'd do, if I ever moved. She'd probably have to invest in cable."

CHAPTER 6

Marsden-Lacey, England

Present Day

Johns walked slowly with the young boy beside him through the nighttime village. Store lights along the main street cast a friendly glow out onto the snow-covered ground. He couldn't help but smile at the seasonal decorations put up by the Marsden-Lacey citizenry.

Most shopkeepers and businesses not only dressed their windows with greenery, but also treated their customers to holiday music ranging from American country songs about sad Christmases to the traditional classics like *Hark The Herald Angels Sing* and Handel's, *Messiah*. Street lamps were wrapped with tree trimmings going right up to below the glass light fixture, giving the impression of each pole wearing a hairy, green ruff around its neck. Johns tried, but he couldn't imagine wanting to be anywhere else at Christmas other than Marsden-Lacey.

As the Chief Detective Inspector, he took a great deal of pride in this village. It was, even for its size, a close-knit community. Most of the pedestrians they met, he recognized or actually knew. His mind was like a vice when it came to remembering things about people, and, as if on cue, two familiar tall, well-dressed men came into view. Alistair Turner and Perigrine Clark, with their dog, Comstock, walked leisurely up the road toward him and Emerson. The four stopped to speak.

"Good evening, Chief," Alistair said smiling. "It's a pleasant night for enjoying the new fallen snow."

Perigrine and Alistair shook hands with the Chief and offered the same greeting to young Emmy, who eagerly joined in on the time-honored male peace ritual of the handshake.

As the older men exchanged pleasantries, Emerson was watching Perigrine particularly closely, causing the tall, sandy blonde man to use the brim of his hat as a shadowing device for his face. Only a couple of months ago, Perigrine saved Emerson from some nasty types, but chose to keep his identity secret by calling himself 'The Fox'. At the time, it was necessary to stay incognito, but it would be awkward to explain The Fox's real identity at this point to the child.

Alistair clicked Comstock's leash making the stocky black schnauzer trot up and wag his tail. This simple distraction worked, switching Emerson's attention to the likable dog.

"Emerson and I are on our way to the village hall," Johns said, giving the boy a pat on the shoulder. "Things are shaping up nicely for the competition next week."

"Did you know, Chief, that Alistair is one of the judges?"

"Excellent choice on Agosto's part. I'd better not be seen by my competitors chatting you up," Johns said affably. "I'm participating, as well. The Constabulary has a team."

Alistair put his hand over his heart. "As a gentleman and a thief, I intend to hold myself to the highest levels of integrity, Chief."

The three men shared a relaxed, knowing, chuckle. Alistair and Perigrine had recently been released from an internment at the Marsden-Lacey Constabulary. They'd been in some trouble with a counterfeiting ring, but their involvement was somehow expunged from the records and they were allowed to go free. Johns liked the two men and enjoyed their company, but he was never sure what was their real story. They shared a thriving garden and landscaping business, but at this time of year, they generally traveled abroad.

"Glad to see you both staying home for the holidays. Usually, you're off to warm climates," Johns said, trying to suss out in a casual way some information about their clandestine traveling practices.

"Perigrine has decided it's the year for him to slow down and enjoy a traditional Christmas. I was invited to be a judge by Señor Agosto for the Marsden-Lacey Pudding and Pie Bake-Off. The Healy chef has been working hard to find enough of us to handle all the teams."

"Do you know the names of the other judges yet?" Johns asked.

"Yes, actually, I do. One of the lady judges is an American. Her name is Lana Chason, a friend of Piers Cousins. She writes for an American culinary magazine. The other one…, I was told today about a woman from London. Let me see…what was her name?" Alistair mused to himself. "Oh, yes, how silly of me. I should have immediately remembered it. Her name was Saundra Johns. Any relationship to you and Polly, Chief?"

Johns jaw dropped perceptibly. Quickly regaining his composure, his face became rigid, but flushed.

"You look like you saw a ghost," Perigrine said, with a touch of concern in his voice. "Are you okay?"

Johns took a deep breath and exhaled forcefully.

"I didn't see a ghost, but I'm pretty sure I felt the icy, heartless grip of a devil squeeze my heart at Alistair's mention of that name."

Perigrine spoke first. "If I may say so, Chief, that reaction can generally be attributed to one of two things when it comes to a man."

Johns shook his head as if trying to comprehend the magnitude of his situation and in a vague way asked, "And what would those two things be?"

"One, a crazy ex-lover he'd rather not ever see again, or two, a woman he wishes he'd never known."

"You hit it on the head, Mr. Turner," Johns said, his eyes cold as steel. "She's both and…she's my wife."

Scene break

Martha stoked the fire in the pretty Delft tiled fireplace. She loved her bedroom. When she first considered buying the canal-side cottage, she hoped the chimneys still worked. They only needed minor repair and during the cold winter nights, she enjoyed nothing so much as lying in her snug bed, surrounded by her pets and listening to the crackling of the tiny fire.

With utter contentment, she soon slept soundly.

Again, she found herself downstairs in her living room, and she heard laughter coming from the kitchen. Wanting to join the party and enticed by the delicious smells of garlic sautéing in butter, Martha got up to follow the scent and the voices. The sounds of people talking and food being prepared, pulled her into the narrow hallway leading to the kitchen, but, as she made it less than half-way down, the laughter stopped and a feeling of unease settled upon her.

Out of nowhere, Helen was behind her. She needed Martha to come with her and to hurry. Helen acted agitated and scared, but Martha was unable to move fast enough to keep up. Helen floated like a ghost backward. She leaned out to Martha to try to grab her, but Martha's hands kept slipping and a sinking sensation took hold of her.

The next thing she knew, she was in a round, stone chamber with completely vertical sides reaching up maybe fifty feet into the air. Trying to find her bearings, she looked around the enclosure, not sure how she'd arrived there. Mocking laughter rang through the tight room, bouncing off the curved surface of the stone forcing her to cover her ears. Looking up to locate the direction of the laughter, Martha realized she must be in a well. Lichen and moss clung to the walls, as water dripped down making a lost, lonely sound. The moon's face hovered above the well's rim undulating, as if reflected through moving water. A face ascended over the circumference of the well's opening.

Soon, Martha saw a dark-haired woman bent over the side and staring down at her. The sound of the slab being worked across the stone top infused Martha with panic. She called to the woman to stop, to not close her in, but soon all the moonlight was gone.

Creeping panic slowly nibbled at her mind. She fought the urge to slip further into its grip. Water on her feet crept slowly up her ankles. The well was filling. She pleaded, "No! Help me, someone!" Treading water, she floated upward to the slab cover. Frantically, she pushed at the stone trying to move it. The water swirled and bubbled around her neck. Breathing room was running out. "Help!" She banged her fists against the slab. "Merriam!"

Completely soaked from sweat, Martha woke up. She lay unmoving looking up at the ceiling. Amos, Gus, and Vera sat on their haunches blinking at her. Her own voice must have brought her out of the dream. Relief spread through her tight muscles and brain. She was safe in her house, in her room, with her three bed-hogs, again, trying to nestle in as close to her as possible. The moonlight filtered into the room and Martha wondered why so many nightmares were visiting her lately.

"What's the deal, guys?" she asked the blanket and pillow thieves. "I feel like I've run a marathon. Why all these nightmares, huh?"

Vera yawned and curled back up in a tight warm ball, while Gus was busy repositioning himself on the pillow by Martha's head. Amos crawled up and put her head right next to Martha's hand. The four-pound fuzz-ball stuck her muzzle under her owner's palm.

"I'm okay, Amos," she assured her furry friend. "I think your human needs to quit eating before bedtime. Wanna crawl in under the covers?"

It wasn't long before Amos, well-tucked between Martha and the inside of her feather duvet, was softly snoring and the two kitties settled back into their long winter's nap. Martha lay there watching the embers glow in her fireplace. Something was stirring her mind's deeper waters. It was almost like a wicked premonition, malignant and moving in slow degrees, toward her.

She chuckled softly to herself at her own theatrics. What she needed was a nice relaxing weekend at a spa hotel like Helen had suggested. They would come back and have fun cooking with

Polly. Martha smiled at the notion of stirring it up with Johns' mother again.

Settled, and the black thoughts of the nightmare extinguished by the closeness of loving friends, Martha rolled over into a fetal position careful to not disturb two cats and one dog, tucked her pillow up around her head and fell into a calm, happy sleep. Morning would soon come to Flower Pot Cottage and with it, an ill wind bringing little good.

CHAPTER 7

Bath, England 1787

"The Story of How Lady Alissa Allen brought Shakespeare to Farthingay House."

Lady Alissa Allen checked and rechecked her jewelry box. The brooch was not there. Only last night at the ball, she'd worn the diamond and ruby brooch given to her by her husband. It was his wedding gift to her and once belonged to his mother, the Baroness. It was priceless.

She tried to declutter her tired mind. If she retraced her steps after the ball, surely her memory would hit on the answer. Resting her pretty, plump hand against her cheek, she stared at herself in the vanity's looking glass, thinking about last evening's dance.

Pleasurable scenes swam up through her still groggy, Chablis soaked brain. Yes, there'd been the wickedly exciting moment when Lord Giles Farthingay pulled her behind the drawing room curtains and told her she was the most beautiful woman he'd ever laid eyes on. He'd put his hands around her waist and his kiss was so long, she almost swooned, and would have, but for his strong arms holding her so tightly. Lady Alissa smiled at herself in the glass. It had been a wonderful night and now a thrilling memory.

A knock on the door made her smile vanish immediately. Sir William Allen, her husband, announced himself.

"Please enter," she said, standing quickly and checking herself to make sure she was presentable.

A much older man, at least, thirty years her senior, poked his grey head around the door. He smiled and asked, "May I come in, my wife?"

She curtsied and did a quick nod of her head as a sign of respect for her husband, "Please do."

Ambling in, he made a direct line to a wingback chair and sat down with a sigh. The short jaunt up a flight of stairs and down a hallway was tiring and he sat for some time before talking. It was decorum to wait for her husband to speak first. She continued to stand until he finally motioned for her to sit down.

"My dear wife," he began, "last night Lord Giles came to me and invited us to attend his ball this coming Friday night. You charmed him last evening and he hoped we would accept his invitation."

Alissa's heart fluttered in her breast, but her expression didn't betray her inner thoughts. To do otherwise would have betrayed her excitement at the possibility of seeing Lord Giles once more.

She answered, however, with wifely modesty and deference to her husband's authority.

"I leave it to you, my husband, to decide if we should attend."

The man was watching his wife's face intently. Lady Alissa sensed something amiss in her husband's demeanor. She knew there was another order of this business, but what was it?

"Lord Giles has a minor request. Would you oblige him, my wife?" her husband asked, never taking his eyes from hers.

A sudden tightness gripped her stomach, as though some form of doom marched toward her.

"And what would his request be?" she asked, her expression perplexed.

A flash of hesitation flicked across her husband's face. She noted it, but it quickly evaporated. "Lord Giles asks that My Lady wear the charming dress from last evening, and not change one aspect of her accoutrements including the diamond and ruby brooch I presented to you on our wedding day."

She blanched. Slowly, the blood drained from her face. Glad to be sitting, she quickly righted herself internally and smiled coolly. Her nostrils flaring ever so imperceptibly, she gave an appreciable portrayal of a woman touched by indignation.

"I find his manner crude. Am I but a courtesan, that I may be entreated to follow any man's request regarding my wardrobe?"

"Not any man's," Sir William said silkily. "I, your husband and the Master of this house, also wish to see you dressed as you were last night."

The verbal slap stung her. She maintained her composure, simply due to her unwillingness to lose the little dignity she was allowed as a woman. However, with no recourse to his demand, Lady Alissa stayed mute and motionless on her vanity stool. Her husband gained his feet and shuffled toward her bedroom door leaving without another word.

Not a woman lacking in her own talents, Lady Alissa waited for the door's latch to catch. To ask her maid about the brooch, would bring suspicion upon herself. The loss of the heirloom would bring questions. If she'd been seen last night in the arms of Lord Giles, most likely, she'd be beaten by her husband, with no reproach from society or the law.

"My Lady?" came her maid's voice from the accompanying room used as a dressing closet.

Lady Alissa turned to see the girl standing in the dressing room door with a folded piece of paper in her hand. "This came for you by messenger a moment ago."

She handed what appeared to be a letter to her mistress.

With shaking hands, Lady Alissa opened the letter. She asked the maid to please give her privacy. The girl dutifully left the same way as Sir William. Alone, Alissa read the words written on the paper. It was unsigned and simply stated that the author knew about her compromising conduct the night before with a certain man of high station, and if she wanted her brooch back, she would need to send a manuscript from her husband's library in exchange.

The letter listed and described a play by Shakespeare, which Lady Alissa recognized. She was to meet the person at the old stone folly at midnight the next evening.

Nothing indicated who the author might be, but by the handwriting and the weight of the paper, she knew it came from someone of means and education. Lady Alissa took the letter over to her fireplace and laid it on the coals, watching as it caught fire and burned completely. Any trace of her misconduct must be destroyed. Her only recourse was to make the meeting. A blackmailer was a parasite that was never satiated. She worked out a plan.

Late the following evening, once the house was asleep, she dressed in clothing she'd removed from the laundry. They were men's britches, a coarse shirt of muslin, hose for her legs and a thick wool jacket the farm laborers used during cold weather. Shoes were more difficult to find. As a lady, her footwear was limited, but she settled on her riding boots as an alternative to silk slippers.

She studied herself in the looking glass and frowned. If she was to succeed, she needed to rough herself up a bit. It came to her. Grabbing some of the debris and soot from the fireplace grate, she covered her face completely. The grey and black from the coal she rubbed under her eyes and up through her auburn hair, provided an excellent disguise as a dirty farm youth.

Winding her hair into a tight bun on the top of her head, she secured it with a pin and topped it off with an old greasy looking hat. Going over to her bed, she picked up a revolver, checked that all was as it should be and stuffed it into one of the deep pockets of her jacket. She slung onto her back, a quiver full of arrows and a bow. Securing them so they couldn't move, she used a slender rope taken from the stables and lowered herself down from her window and onto the ground below.

The night was chilly and Lady Alissa decided to be at the folly long before whoever else might arrive. She'd taken the precaution with her maid to leave her alone all night, claiming to have a headache and wishing to not be disturbed at any cost. Lord William never troubled her with any of her wifely duties. He kept to his room at the other end of the house and was always asleep each night right after supper.

Open fields under a bright starlit sky helped to clear her mind. She rehearsed her plan to secure her brooch. The manuscript requested was concealed in her tight bodice under double wrappings encircling her breasts to hide her natural female shape.

Arriving at the folly, she considered the layout of the structure and its surroundings. With quick, decisive movements, she pulled herself up into a thick fir tree that acted as a spatial counterbalance to the architecture. Since it was only about eleven o'clock, she would have to wait.

Grateful the wind was still, she spent a restless hour before catching sounds of human movement approaching across the hard ground. Her heart beat hard within her chest. It was a man's stride, she was sure. Soon he was visible to her and she watched to see if he was alone.

First, he inspected the folly and finding no one, he came to stand on the small portion of land along the building's front end overlooking the lake. Lady Alissa watched him for some time, assessing his movements for signs of weakness. He looked tall and well built. She kept a sharp outlook for other helpers he might have brought along as backup.

The man turned from gazing at the water, and in an instant, the moonlight shown down on his face. She recognized him. It was Lord Giles himself. Thinking this might be useful, she prepared herself mentally for their first foray.

In a voice she tried to disguise as a man's by talking lower and more forcefully, she said, "I'm here to collect my lady's brooch."

Lord Giles spun around trying to locate the direction of the call. He peered into the darkness. Nothing stirred.

"Who's there?" he commanded.

She watched his face with the moonlight illuminating his handsome features. It was a pity, she thought, that she might have to kill him.

"Drop the brooch or I'll drop you," she bluffed. Her voice sounding tougher and more masculine each time she spoke. A tiny grin hovered at the corners of her mouth. She was enjoying herself.

On the ground, Farthingay turned to face the talking tree. A huge, roguish smile spread across his face. "Come down here and take it from me," he called back. Settling both of his hands on his hips in a jaunty gesture of defiance, he stood waiting for an answer.

Lady Alissa had hung her quiver on a secure branch so as to have it ready. With the bow in her grasp, she gently pulled its string, setting an arrow and took aim at the feather in Farthingay's hat. A twinkle in her eye, she gripped the arrow and pulled it back letting it fly. It hissed and sped through the air lifting Farthingay's hat from his head and landing it effortlessly upon the lake's calm, tranquil surface where it stayed afloat.

The gentleman looked completely undone. His arms first flung themselves up to his naked head and dropped like limp, empty flour sacks to his sides.

"What in Hell do you think you're doing?" he shouted at the tree.

"Show me the brooch," the tree demanded and I won't put the next one in your fleeing arse."

Lady Alissa barely suppressed a giggle at her growing command of the masculine vernacular.

Lord Giles stood dumbstruck. He reached into an inner recess of his coat and produced the brooch, which he showed to the tree. "See it?"

"Put it on the folly's pediment. You'll have to climb a bit, but you look fit...enough." Lady Alissa quietly readied another arrow and took aim.

Farthingay didn't move. He watched the tree. "Have you the manuscript?"

"I don't deal with blackmailers," Lady Alissa stated and let loose the second arrow. It seared through the air right beside Farthingay's left ear. "I'll happily pierce it for you the next time."

Being bested, his appreciation for Lady Alissa's champion was apparent. He climbed the stone masonry and sat the brooch upon the pediment's cornice. Jumping down, he performed a deep bow to the tree.

"Better be on your way, Farthingay," Lady Alissa instructed. "I'm nearly out of arrows, but I've saved one last means of instruction, if you test me. I promise it will warm your walk home tonight."

She couldn't help appreciating his good looks and his good humor at his own loss. As he disappeared into the night and his footsteps became lost to her ears, she decided to wait for at least another hour before decamping from her tree.

Finally, feeling stiff from the cold, she gingerly let herself down from the fir tree. Being careful to stay out of the moonlight, she made her way to the folly and climbed the stonework with ease. Right where she'd instructed Farthingay to put it, lay the brooch. She tucked it quickly into her pocket and secured the button. It was time to hurry home.

As she ascended the hillside with the majestic, stone Georgian house in view, Alissa took in her surroundings. Her husband's family had owned the estate for less than one hundred years, a short period of time for the English gentry. Her mother had made the match with Sir William, telling Alissa how lucky she was to be marrying a wealthy man with a title. Alissa's family was far wealthier in comparison to Sir William; however, her parents had too many daughters for which to find husbands, making for scant marital opportunities for the young ladies further down the line in age. Alissa, being the last one of twelve, had to accept whatever was thrown her way. Her only brother would inherit everything leaving marriage the only alternative for her and her sisters.

Catching a movement in the trees off to her left, Lady Alissa turned around in time to see a man running straight for her. Lord Giles had her in less than a second and together they fell to the ground. She struggled and tried to free herself from his grasp, but he held her far too tightly. Her hat fell from her head and the pinned-up auburn hair slipped its restraints, falling around her face.

"You?" he said and laughed. "I should spank your backend for all the trouble you've given me tonight."

Alissa continued to fight against him. She freed one of her arms and pulled his hair and slapped his face with her hand.

"Where did you learn to shoot like that?" he asked in between slaps and fending off her hair pulling.

"My brother," she grunted, trying to use her knees to bludgeon his lower extremities.

He twisted and flipped her over on her back. With more strength at his command, he easily managed to hold both her wrists with one of his own hands and sit on her using his legs to quell her flailing.

"I'm going to sit here until you calm down. Once you're done trying to kill me, we can talk. Let me know when you're ready," he said.

Alissa was furious. A few more savage attempts at freeing herself were dealt out, but soon she lay still, yet refusing to look him in the face.

"I hate you," was all she said.

"I don't hate you," he replied. "In fact, I think I love you."

Alissa huffed at this ridiculous revelation.

"I haven't a farthing to my name and, I'm pretty sure, neither does your husband...any longer," Lord Giles said.

With this last remark, he owned Alissa's full attention. "What do you mean?" she demanded.

"If I get up, do you promise to sit still and not run off?"

She considered him for a moment. "I'll listen, but with great reservation. The confessions of a common thief hold little weight."

"Why do you think you're even out here tonight?" he asked. "Your doddering husband asked me to steal the brooch from you last night. He intends to be rid of you, but not before he commands a payment from your brother to keep quiet about your adulterous behavior."

Alissa was stunned. She quickly remembered, however, her husband's unusual behavior the morning he told her about Lord Giles' ball. His lack of interest in her and how most likely he'd only married her for her dowery also lent weight to what Farthingay had said. But to throw her out and mangle her name by accusing her of adultery was beyond anything she'd ever conceived of.

"Are you going to take the brooch from me?" she asked in a haughty voice.

Lord Giles took her hand and held it. He pulled her into an upright position and stared at her gloved hand for a long time. At last, he said, "No. I don't want it. It's yours. I want to apologize for last night. The minute I laid eyes on you at the dance, I wanted *you,* not the damn brooch. That's why I kissed you. I only went along with this whole charade because I hoped he'd toss you out and I could have you for myself."

Lady Alissa, for the second time that night, realized how attractive Farthingay was. She removed her hand gently from his and sighed at her own confusing situation.

"I'm not sure what to do next. I have a husband who wants to be rid of me, even to the tune of having me declared an adulterer, and I have a blackguard who says he loves me." She turned to Farthingay and their eyes met. He leaned over and tenderly took her chin, lifting it.

"May I?"

Something inside her chest lifted with the thrill of his closeness. She gave one nod and he leaned in, softly kissing her. In truth, it had only been the second time she'd been kissed by a man. The first time belonged to him, as well.

They stayed that way for a long time and when they broke, he gently held her chin as he addressed her.

"Any woman who can shoot like you do, climb a tree, and nearly beat me within an inch of my life is, in my eyes, a treasure beyond gold. I think you owe Sir William his brooch, my lady, and, if you're up for it, I need a partner to come with me to Barbados. I've got a business there, and I need the talents of a quick mind and an even quicker hand such as yours. What do you say?"

Lady Alissa smiled broadly at his proposal. Never had any man deemed to treat her with this kind of consideration. Her options were sadly unequal. Staying with Sir William would, sooner or later, end up in a complete disaster for her. Marriage for a woman in the 1700's was fraught with abuse, both physical and mental, the wife lacking in legal protection and dependent on the man's notion of integrity and morality. In England, wives were still sold in the public market, if their husbands had tired of them or found another woman they wished to take up with.

Any insinuations by Lord William that Alissa was a woman of loose morals allowed him to put her away, and her brother and her family would turn their backs on her forever. She would be socially and financially ruined. The decision of whether to go or not with Farthingay was a moot point.

"Why are you going to Barbados?" she asked him.

"There's a nice trade in other nation's resources, legally questionable tis true, but one in which a man might make a secure fortune if he's up to the task. I want to save my inheritance and my own estate. This business is dangerous, but highly profitable."

"I'm not giving Sir William his brooch back," Alissa said. "And for that matter, I'm no longer Lady Alissa Allen. I've no hope for a divorce, but if you're serious about your offer, I'm willing to take you up on it."

She offered her hand to Farthingay. He took it, raised it to his lips, and kissed it.

"You are *my* Lady Farthingay and once we make our fortune, I'll sue Parliament for your divorce. Till that time, if you'll have me, I want you as my wife, not as my mistress."

Alissa grabbed Farthingay in a very unladylike hug around his neck and kissed him fully on the mouth. He wrapped his arms around her, laughing at her forwardness.

"You're a minx and I'm damned lucky to have you."

Two years later, Lady Alissa Allen inherited all of Sir William's property upon his death. She'd been considered abducted since the night of her disappearance from her husband's home. A deputy minister found her living in Barbados and apprised her of the fortune waiting for her in England. She left the island one week later along with a companion and chaperone who presented himself for her voyage, a man of means and title, Lord Giles Farthingay.

Once back in England, the Allen estate was sold and its contents auctioned. The new Lady Alissa Farthingay, along with her husband, Lord Giles lived many more happy years together, at his home, Greenwoods Abbey. Their children thrived and their love survived old age. Shakespeare's foul copies, once used as barter between greedy Allen and gallant Farthingay, stayed safe and secure for many centuries to come within their family's magnificent library.

CHAPTER 8

"By the pricking of my thumbs,

Something wicked this way comes."

-Shakespeare, MacBeth, Act IV, Scene I

Marsden-Lacey, England

Present Day

"I don't carry my own bags," the petite dark-haired woman was saying. "That's what I pay people like you to do." She watched the young man struggle with her three suitcases and one corpulent makeup satchel, as they ascended the stairs of the hotel. It pleased her to point out that she was his better. Everyone had a place in life, and Saundra loved to remind others of theirs while pointing out the loftiness of her own.

"Yes, Madam," he said compliantly. As they reached her room, he asked, "Is there anything else, Madam?"

She scrunched up her face at the hotel room's decor. Being accustomed to her own excessive self-worth and the diligence required of her to keep up appearances, she wasn't pleased about having to slum-it in such a shabby place. If other people were to see her staying here, they might not willingly believe she was as wonderful as she really was.

"I guess not," she mumbled. "Oh, yes, where can I find a skinny latte in this backwater? You do know what that is, don't you?"

"Try Harriet's Tea Shoppe or The Traveller's Inn." The boy put out his hand for a tip, and the woman gave him coins amounting to about an English pound she'd found in her coat pocket.

The young steward turned his back to her and rolled his eyes. He let himself out of the room without a 'thank you', leaving the woman alone. She stood up and walked over to one of the windows overlooking High Street. Down below, people came and went along the sidewalk, but Saundra Johns wasn't interested in their lives. In fact, she was rarely interested in other people at all unless they had something to offer her. She turned away from the spectacle of holiday cheerfulness. Her gaze fell upon her darling makeup satchel. This made her smile.

Unzipping the flap, the satchel rolled open displaying a plethora of small enclosures full of eye pencils, different colors of foundations, multiple shades of lipsticks, and every expensive beauty product offered by London's many chic, upscale department stores.

Lovingly, Saundra pulled out different items that caught her eye. There were things to make her eyelashes longer, creams to remove the hair over her lip, and brushes to sculpt her makeup like a painter might use to paint a portrait.

With joy, she remembered the small case of jewelry she'd also packed. Quickly she went over to her bags and rifled through them until she found the jewelry. It always gave her such pleasure to arrange her beauty items, her jewelry and her clothes in any place she might be staying. The ritual made her feel like she had something solid, something to ground her. Though she couldn't put her finger on what it was that made her life always seem to be missing something, she knew that the time she spent in front of the mirror made her happy. Her reflection was her favorite place. It was her home.

A knock on her room door startled her. "I wonder who it could be," she mumbled as she went to the door and peeped through the tiny eyehole. A wintery smile played at the corners of her red-stained lips. Their blood color hinted at the owner's predilection for fresh meat.

"Come in, Merriam," Saundra said, opening the door. She made way for the Chief, letting him come fully into the room. He appeared uncomfortable and this pleased her.

"Saundra," he said, "I thought I would come by and say hello. I heard last night you were to be one of the judges for our Bake-Off."

"Have you been hanging around the hotel all day, Merriam, waiting for me to show? How sweet of you to rush up and welcome me," she said in a simpering, singsong tone. "It's been a while. What do you think of my new hairstyle?" She coyly maneuvered a pose she knew showed her body to its best advantage, while watching Johns' expression the entire time.

Saundra Johns believed in her looks. They'd never let her down. When mixed with her own subtle allusions to her frailty and tininess, her beauty's power was limitless. Men loved doing things for her. They lifted things, they fetched things, and they paid for things. She was their queen, and they paid homage to her. If they ever winced or struggled under her dominion, she tweaked them back into compliance by pouting or getting weaker.

The problem with Saundra was, she thought they did it because they adored her, or that they should do it to prove they adored her. The truth was, they did it because she appealed to their own vanity or to their desire to believe in her rhetoric. Most of the men learned the truth the hard way. After empty years of opening one vein after another to appease her bottomless self-obsession, they were cast aside, and most, like Merriam Johns, were left with an aching hole in their heart and lingering trust issues in future relationships.

It took ten years for Johns to realize, and accept, his marriage to Saundra was only ever going to be a one-way street. She was a narcissist. He'd loved her, but it was an empty, lonely existence, so he'd asked for a divorce. She'd never given it.

"I came by to talk with you," Johns said. "Why did you come back to Marsden-Lacey, Saundra?"

She sensed something different in her husband's tone and she didn't like it. There wasn't the tiniest hint of attraction or longing in his voice. This incensed her, so she played her hand. Like any good surgeon about to carve on a living body, she checked to see if the heart muscle was strong and resilient.

"I came back to see you. I love you, Merriam and I want to make our marriage work."

His reaction wasn't what she expected. He blanched and shifted his stance, indicating his discomfort. Ignoring her bland testament to their love, he paused before responding.

"Is that why you haven't signed the divorce papers? I've been waiting for them for two years. You can't keep putting this off, Saundra. My lawyer says you can't contest it any longer."

Anger and indignation vied for top position. She'd pulled out her best card. Tears streamed down her face, not at the loss of her husband, but at the need to make him pay, make him squirm.

"I won't give it to you, Merriam," she hissed.

"You will. You have to," he said evenly.

Saundra's tears dried up instantly. A new thought occurred to her. She walked over to him and looking him straight in the eyes, she asked with a lethal evenness to her voice, "Is there someone else?"

"Yes."

Saundra recoiled from the simplicity of his answer like a vampire shown a crucifix. She waited for him to elaborate, but he offered nothing.

"Do you love her?" she asked in a demanding, mocking tone.

"I'm not going to discuss that," he countered. "You walked out five years ago and have had multiple lovers. What do you want? It must be something or you wouldn't be here."

She didn't want Merriam back. It only galled her that he might have a life outside of her. She considered the situation and decided the only pleasure left to her was making him see how he should have never mistreated her, never shifted his slavish adoration from her to someone else. That was an unfortunate, stupid mistake on his part, so he deserved what he was about to get.

She turned her back on him and flippantly said, "I've talked with my solicitor, and he advises me to try and work out a settlement. I want you to sell the farm. The money from the sale should be divided between us equally."

"That is my home. It has been in our family for nearly two centuries. My mother has her business there. I won't sell it."

His tone was unemotional, but she saw she'd won the desired reaction. If you can't have complete control over someone, having their hatred is second best. It meant you were able to incite their emotions, and that was power, too.

Saundra supped on his anger. She drank it in, but feigned indifference at his upset. This action was intended to belittle him further by showing how his feelings unaffected her, how negligible they were to her.

"Well, that's too bad. I need the money. I always need money, darling. I'm your wife and the house is by rights mine in equal share. If you want your divorce, be prepared to sell the dear old farm. Mother Johns can make her moonshine somewhere else."

Though her back was turned to him, she smelled his hatred, his loathing and his rage. It was excruciatingly thrilling to her. She didn't fear him because she was acutely aware of being the only predator in the room. Instead, she moved toward the door.

"I'm busy, Merriam. I have a little food contest to judge. Charity is so close to my heart. You'd better get back to your local lady love. Hope she's not some toothless rube, but most likely she is, since she likes to live in such a dull, drab country place."

Saundra opened her door. Merriam walked out. She didn't bother with goodbyes or reflecting on the retreating figure of the only man who'd ever loved her. She simply shut the door and went back to setting up her beauty products, makeup and nail polishes along the fragile, hotel glass shelves and the cramped sink area of the bathroom.

It was time for a nice long soak, a hot cup of tea, a skin tightening facial and dreams about acquiring money, preferably other people's.

CHAPTER 9

Martha and Helen were up early that morning and their things were packed. Polly was going to stay at Martha's cottage to watch the pets. She said it would be nice to have the place to herself to work on the team's menus for the competition.

The trip to Lord Percy Farthingay's estate, Greenwoods Abbey, would only take about two hours, and afterwards, they were to stay at a nice manor house hotel, The Brentmore. It had all the relaxing perks, like hot sauna's, massage treatments, fluffy beds and pretty bedrooms. Piers was to meet them tonight at the hotel. Martha decided seeing a new client wasn't a total waste, especially if it meant she might enjoy a spa experience as a follow-up treat.

They found Greenwoods. As they pulled in through the entrance gates, they became increasingly aware that the entire place was succumbing to neglect. Hedgerows were chocked with weeds and invasive trees popped up through their tops. The very road, itself, looked as if few cars ever passed along its tracks.

"This is creepy," Martha said, her eyes wide with delight. "I've lived in England a long time and this is the first time I can say I've ever seen a place so overgrown and deteriorated. You'd kind of expect a Lord to live in something like Piers' Healy House."

Helen sounding upbeat, said, "It's so old, and maybe Lord Percy is strapped for money. That's probably why we're here, if you want to know the truth. We'll soon find out, though."

Martha's mind was working its way down its favorite paths lined with hidden mysteries, gothic melodramas, and criminal underworlds. "I don't know, Helen. This might be a trick by some lunatic to get two beautiful women out to this remote place and lock us up in one of his long-forgotten, dusty, decrepit wings of the house."

"You sound like that docudrama you love to watch. What's it called? *Creepy Criminals*?" Helen asked.

"It's *Crimes, Creeps and Cribs*, Helen," Martha said sounding put out by Helen's lack of a grasp on current popular television shows. "Last week they did a story on this very thing. A woman was held captive in an insane asylum during the Victorian era. She went mad finally and her ghost haunts the abandoned building to this day."

"We're here," Helen announced, pulling the car up to the front door of the Jacobean-style house. Red brick cladding and mullioned windows with three-dimensional elements like turrets, gables and window bays set the house well within the time of James I.

"I wouldn't be surprised if the library of Lord Percy did have works by Shakespeare. The period of the architecture is perfect," Helen said.

Martha scanned the ruinous state of the house with its weed beds for gardens and crumbling turrets that looked ready to topple down on the first person to try the doorbell. "It's perfect all right--perfect for being chased by some Victorian crazy lady with sharp nails and dark circles around her eyes."

"Would you stop it!" Helen hissed. "You're giving me the shivers with all your talk. What is it with you lately? You've got to stop watching all those horror films and crime shows. That's probably where the nightmares are coming from."

Helen took a calming, deep breath and finished in a more gentle tone. "No more wacky, weird tales of floating fiends. We've got to be prepared for some eccentricity, by the looks of things, and some need for antihistamine tablets. The place is probably rife with mold. Are we ready?"

They made it to the top of the front steps of Greenwoods. Helen reached for the doorbell but gave Martha one more minute to pull her brain back from the abyss of the gothic.

"I'm ready, but if the person who answers the door looks even remotely like Lon Chaney, I'm out of here. Got it?" Martha said, holding her pinky up for Helen to seal the deal by locking theirs together.

Helen rolled her eyes and linked her pinky with Martha's giving it a half-hearted shake. "It's like I'm working with Gidget."

"Helen, do you know what I like best about you?" Martha asked.

"What?" Helen's hand poised to pull the bell rope.

"You've been chased by mobsters, shot at by a lunatic, and locked in a freezer, but you always bounce back…to your pragmatic, professional, perfectly coiffed self. You're solid, Helen, completely, one hundred percent solid."

Helen gave the bell rope a hard tug. She considered Martha through half-slit eyes and pursed her lips into a pucker.

"I'm going to hurt you, if you attempt to start a conversation regarding locked up Victorians, criminal masterminds, or evil fiends lurking behind the wainscoting."

Martha shot dirty looks at the back of Helen's perfectly coiffed head. The door opened and a meek girl dressed in a simple black skirt and white blouse stood blinking at them. Raising her hand to her brow to shade her eyes, she studied the two women for a few seconds.

"I'm sorry," she apologized, "but I'm having a difficult time with my eyes. The light outside is so bright."

The girls gave her a moment to adjust and as they announced who they were, she asked them to follow her inside. As soon as the door shut behind them, they understood the girl's earlier difficulty. The entire house was completely dark. No natural light filtered into the rooms, halls, or landings as they followed their guide deeper into the interior of the house.

"One moment, please," the girl said, as they reached a stopping point. "I'll let Lord Percy's nephew, Mr. Brickstone, know you are here." She indicated a seating area a few feet away. Martha and Helen smiled and walked the short distance to a settee Queen Elizabeth I might have sat on as a child. The place was oppressively musty, and, though it was impressive in size, it resembled something in which Miss Havisham would be comfortable.

"Helen," Martha whispered, her tone confident. "If we need it, I brought my mace."

Helen's eyes shifted carefully from the long gallery to look Martha square in the face.

"Good. Something about this place has the hair on the back of my neck prickling."

The sound of a door opening brought the girls to their feet. A tall man walked toward them out of the gloom. As his features became more distinct, they saw he was attractive, polished-looking and in his late forties.

"Mrs. Ryes, so nice to finally meet you. Thank you for coming all this way." Mr. Brickstone took Helen's offered hand, holding it a bit too long while he checked her out overtly from head to toe. Extricating her hand after a few awkward seconds, Helen turned to introduce Martha.

"This is my colleague, Mrs. Littleword."

Addressing his attention only to Martha's breasts, he said, "It *is* a pleasure."

Martha took his offered hand and shook it saying, "Yes, the other white meat."

His gaze snapped up to her eyes, and looking at her a bit befuddled as if not sure of what she'd said, he quickly righted himself and asked the two women to follow him back down the corridor.

They walked along a number of hallways and descended a stairwell where the plaster was chipping from the walls. He chatted along the way about the many unusual architectural novelties the house held.

"This wing was added about one hundred years after the original building was built. The Lord at the time wanted to create a suitable library and the main house was lacking the proper space. As generations came and went, they added their own mark to the structure. That's why it's a bit rambling. Here we are."

Martha poked Helen in the arm and mouthed the words, "Weirdo. We should leave."

Helen returned the silent statement with a terse headshake and wide round eyes, indicating Martha should desist with any further antics. They continued following him until he finally stopped at an intricately carved entryway.

He pushed on a heavy door with a lovely brass knob. Standing aside, Mr. Brickstone made way for Helen and Martha to pass by him. The room they walked into was magnificent. Early Jacobean, its proportions were rectangular, with three walls housing beautiful built-in bookcases made out of mahogany. Above the cases rose a surface of plaster about six feet tall where a variety of armorial items hung. The ceiling was exquisite in its carved wooden moldings and plasterwork culminating in an imposing family crest in the center. No matter where the eye rested, one was reminded of a timeless beauty an earlier age of wealthy aristocrats sought to achieve in the decorative lavishness of their homes.

"What a treat to visit and see this library. Will we have the pleasure to meet Lord Percy?" Martha asked, turning to address their host.

This particular room boasted tall windows along one side, broken only by a massive fireplace centered between them. Light from their uncovered transoms poured gently down from above. Martha saw Brickstone's features much clearer now, and she noticed, for the first time, a palm-sized birthmark on his neck. Something about it plucked at a corner of her memory.

"No, I'm sorry, Mrs. Littleword. My uncle is ill. He is suffering from dementia these days." Brickstone turned his attention up to the rafters. "This room has given me so much pleasure. Let me show you the manuscript I've brought you such a long distance to see."

He put on a pair of white cotton gloves and motioned for Helen and Martha to join him at a long table where many books, documents and trinkets lay. Helen reached inside her jacket pocket and put on her own white gloves. Brickstone stepped aside to allow the two women to see what lay before them. Several clearly old manuscript were presented for them to inspect.

"I think this is beyond rare, ladies. I want it authenticated and valued. You come highly recommended by my dear friend Bishop Wellerton."

Helen didn't speak. Martha stood back to give her space to breathe. When Helen was focused, a sonic boom wouldn't stir her. Initially, the room was heavy with the lack of sound, and a feeling of timelessness permeated the space. Her hearing adjusted to the tomb-like silence and she begin to make out the barely audible, yet rhythmic, ticking of an ancient grandfather clock sitting at one end of the long room. Nothing and no one moved.

Finally, Helen was done with her appraisal. She stood up from her bent position over the table and reached for a handkerchief in her pocket. Her eyes were glassy.

"Mrs. Ryes, can I get you anything?" Mr. Brickstone asked, his tone solicitous.

"No," she said throatily. She cleared her throat. "I'm a bit overwhelmed by what is before us on this table. It's priceless and should be kept in a fireproof vault. It needs to be looked at by at least two other experts, but I do believe you may have an original foul copy, or original working copy, of one of Shakespeare's plays. My suggestion is to contact your insurance company and ask how they secure items of national, excuse me, global value."

"Will you arrange it for me," Brickstone asked quietly.

Martha immediately noticed that Helen wasn't expecting this response from him. To her credit, she didn't stumble, and instead, said, "I can arrange to have it collected by an armored car and transported to a vault at your bank."

Mr. Brickstone shook his head. "Ultimately, I want it evaluated and sent to auction. I don't want any attention drawn to myself or this estate. My uncle isn't well. I trust you, and I want someone from Sotheby's or Christie's to value it for auction. You make the arrangements. I want this handled with discretion and the auction catalogue to state the seller as private. My uncle's attorney is available for you to speak with regarding the possible sale of any items of the estate. We are trying to raise money to repair so many neglected aspects of the house and lands. I've been given full authority to handle my uncle's affairs."

Helen looked out of her depth. She turned to Martha and said, "Martha, I left my phone in the car. Would you please get it for me? I'll put this manuscript into a Mylar bag while you're gone."

"Sure, Helen. Mr. Brickstone, I'll need help finding my way back. Is there someone who could show me?"

He smiled brightly and walking over to another desk, picked up what appeared to be a walkie-talkie.

"Denise? Denise, please come to the library. I need you to show our guest to her car. Thank you." He put the hand-held device back into its charging station and laughed. "It'll take her some time to walk here."

Both Helen and Martha smiled, but Martha sensed Helen's discomfort with the situation. Soon the meek girl who had greeted them at the front door arrived. Martha followed her out of the library, feeling uncomfortable with leaving Helen behind.

The long paneled and carpeted hallway had windows shuttered along one side. Martha thought it wouldn't hurt to ask Denise if there was a reason for the murky, lightless house.

"Do you keep the curtains drawn to protect the fragile items in the house?" she asked.

"Yes, I guess so, but it's been this way since I came to service here about six months ago," the girl replied.

Martha noted the time frame. "It's such a massive place. Do you ever get a twinge of fright walking around by yourself?"

Denise smiled. Her face lit up at Martha's question. "It can be a bit nervy at times. There's only myself, Mrs. Norton who does the cooking and a nurse named Miss Sutherland. Nellie, I mean Mrs. Norton, and I don't run into Miss Sutherland much, but it can come as a shock when you're alone in one of these passages and someone else is knocking about in another wing."

Martha shivered. "You're a brave young woman, Denise. My imagination would get the better of me in a place like this."

As if on cue, a man's cry came echoing down the passageway. Both women stopped in mid-stride.

"What is that?" Martha whispered.

Denise waited a moment. She appeared to be listening intently. Another burst of moaning, louder this time, rang along the dusty corridor.

"That's Lord Percy. He suffers from dementia and Miss Sutherland, his nurse, is probably helping him with something he doesn't want to do or understand."

Denise didn't appear to be bothered by the moaning. She kept on with her errand of showing Martha to the front of the house. Martha stayed mute until they reached the entryway.

"I think I can find my way back, Denise. Thank you for showing me to the entrance."

The maid left the door ajar and disappeared back into the house's gloom. Martha retrieved the phone and hurried through the empty, lonely maze of halls. Too late, she realized she was lost. A coolness enveloped her and a sudden unease took hold in her mind.

Recognizing her predilection for over indulging her imagination, she told herself to stay calm. Up ahead, she made out the end of the hallway. A draft or a fluttering of the curtains over a long window at the hall's end enabled a thin shaft of light to peek through from the outside. Martha watched transfixed as the movement of the air caused the beam of light to grow. As the curtain parted further, she could finally see.

She'd made only a small misstep in her journey to the library, so with a quick turnaround, she walked in the correct direction. A feeling of gratitude for the thoughtful assistance shown her by either nature or something else made Martha say quietly, "Thank you."

Hurrying on, she soon found herself opening the door to the library once again. Helen and Mr. Brickstone were laughing, but Helen's laugh sounded hollow and insincere. Brickstone was extremely close, too close, his hand pawed her back.

"Here's Martha," Helen said, and with a look of relief and gratitude, she moved hurriedly toward Martha with her hand out to accept the phone. "Thank you for getting the phone. We were talking about Piers and the tennis tournaments he has each year at Healy House. Mr. Brickstone isn't sure if Lord Percy has met him."

Martha handed Helen the phone and said to Brickstone, "Do you play? It looks like you are the type to keep your hand in."

He smirked. "No, I suffer of late from a sensitivity to light. When I go out, I wear special glasses. The intensity of the malady has increased over the years so I stay indoors during the day."

Martha inwardly cringed. She could tell he was lying. He had a tan, but even so, the man exuded a ghoulish quality. She wished they could leave. Helen excused herself to make a call. Martha heard part of her conversation about times and a bank manager. Something again needled her memory.

"Have you lived in England long, Mrs. Littleword?" he asked.

She came back quickly from her mental digging. "Yes, I met my husband here when I was young. We married and my daughter attends Oxford."

"Are you new to working with Mrs. Ryes?"

"Yes, our working arrangement is about six months old. I worked for years as a paralegal."

The man's expression became still and his gaze hung briefly on Martha's face. He turned his attention to the manuscripts and other items lying on his desk. Martha stayed quiet after their brief interchange of personal information. She turned her attention to Helen's phone conversation, as it was coming to an end.

Helen, with perfect professionalism, explained the next steps of their arrangement to Brickstone.

"We have the use of Hisox Insurers and your contact is a dear friend of mine, Sinead Peters. She'll answer any questions you may have about your manuscript's location. I'll wait until we have a firm idea of when the scholars and auction appraisers can make their evaluations before I contact you and meet with your solicitor."

Helen handed Brickstone a piece of paper with the names and numbers.

"An armored transport will be here at ten o'clock in the morning. You may give them the manuscript and they'll deliver it to Sinead at Hisox Insurers. Do you have any questions for me?" Helen asked Brickstone.

"No, this is perfect. Allow me to show you ladies out and I hope you have a wonderful time at The Brentmore Hotel. It has a well-stocked wine cellar and I recommend the steak tartare."

With their business concluded, everyone journeyed back to the front of the house. Helen chatted about when she might expect to connect with one of the most noted Shakespearean scholars, Sir Barstow, and that she hoped to let Mr. Brickstone know something soon.

Martha quietly followed in the back trying to shake off the suggestion of eating raw beef for dinner that evening. She wondered for the last time, as they reemerged into the natural world of blessed light and fresh air, if maybe Brickstone wasn't actually Count Dracula operating under a new alias and using fake tan from a can.

"Thank you, Mr. Brickstone," Helen said at the door before exiting. "We'll talk soon."

When the doors to Greenwood shut behind them, all that was left to do was to settle themselves in Helen's Mercedes and find their way to the Brentmore Hotel.

"Was that weird or what?" Martha stated more than asked.

"That was so weird, I'm not sure if I'm even comfortable being involved in the whole undertaking. He's odd."

"He's a freaking Count Dracula from Looneyville," Martha exclaimed.

"Something was off in there, Martha."

"Here's the creepy thing, while you were in the library tomb with Vlad, I was listening to the moans and screams from his elderly uncle being ministered to by some Nurse Ratchet who's the keeper of the undead."

"What?" Helen blurted, turning her head briefly. It was always good to get a visual to estimate the exaggeration level of Martha's stories.

"Yeah. Supposedly, Uncle, the Lord Farthingay, or whatever his name is, has dementia and doesn't like his bath or wearing clothes. It made me want to bolt the minute I heard his moaning. The maid, Denise, acted like it was a regular day at the mad house."

Helen stared at the gravel road the car was traveling on, not saying a word. She gave the gas pedal a firm press making the car increase its speed.

"Why do I get the feeling we're in another mess?" she asked, her tone annoyed.

Martha flipped the vent blowing warm air from the heater up away from her face. "Hot flash, Helen. Lately, these things kick in if I'm even remotely emotional."

"I know. I hate those things."

They were quiet for a minute, watching the landscape begin to change from desolate and sinister to pastures covered in snow and houses nestled into hills and vales.

"We'll be fine, Helen. It's Christmas, our kids will be with us soon, and Piers and Johns have our backs. No more bad thoughts. Let's go get something yummy to eat." Martha thought about Brickstone's steak tartare recommendation. "Something warm and cooked all the way through."

CHAPTER 10

The Brentmore Hotel was fabulously posh. Helen's Mercedes was whisked away to its own stable and the girls were shown to their rooms. Martha's featured a pretty canopy bed with Colefax and Fowler's Briar Rose fabric which she loved and Helen's employed a Louis Fifteenth French-style upholstered bed done in a blue toile.

"How do you like it?" Helen asked, obviously pleased with herself at picking the perfect room for Martha.

"I love it!" Martha exclaimed. She was using a wooden step stool to get into the tall bed. "I don't want to leave."

"We don't have to for two whole days, so take a nap, get a massage or order that cheese plate you so wanted. I'm off to take a long, hot soak. Have you seen the baths yet? They're so deep. Don't bother me for a least two hours. Ta!"

Helen was gone. Since their rooms connected, she simply popped out and closed the adjoining doors. Martha lay staring up into the exquisitely formed fabric sunburst on the ceiling of the canopy.

"How do they do that?" she muttered. Shutting her eyes, she soon drifted off to sleep only to be awakened by a knocking at her door.

Martha's eyes focused in the dimly lit room. She realized she'd been asleep for a while.

"Martha," Helen's voice called from the other side of the door. "You still asleep?"

"Hang on, Helen. I'm almost there."

Feeling her way off the pedestal for the bed, she groped for the doorknob and opened the door. "I guess I fell asleep. What time is it?"

"Your cheeks are rosy. That sleep did you good." Helen was dressed in a simple black dress with pearls at her neck. Her short auburn hair was tucked behind her ears giving her a sophisticated look. There was a certain sparkle animating her face. "Piers is here. Will you join us for dinner in about an hour? I'm going down for cocktails."

Martha reached up with both hands to inspect the condition of her hair.

"It's going to take some time, kid. Give me an hour for sure. I'll be down for dinner, but not for cocktails. I'll text you."

Helen gave Martha a hug and reached up to give her mussed-up red hair an additional roughing.

"What's that for?" Martha asked still groggy from her wonderful nap.

"I just love you. You're the sister I never had. I'll see you in a bit."

Martha stood in her doorway smiling sappily as her new best buddy walked down the corridor. She shut the door and toddled off to the bath wishing Helen would make her kids come to England for Christmas.

Scene Break

"I've missed you," Piers said. His eyes sparkled with warmth in the candlelight. The cozy, wainscoted cocktail area was dimly lit by electric brass sconces with gold trimmed black shades. Soft laughter tinkled through the room as other guests talked, laughed and enjoyed their drinks and appetizers. The wait staff moved noiselessly and didn't hover. Helen and Piers were sitting in a snug niche by the dark oak-mantled inglenook fireplace, which was perfectly stoked to a crackling blaze.

"I've missed you, too," Helen said smiling brightly. She couldn't help herself from feeling warm, happy and excited to see him again. He was, as always, delicious to look at, tall and dark-haired, with a light sprinkling of grey at the temples making him, if even possible, even more handsome. For better or worse, Piers Cousins always attracted women's attention.

"You look beautiful tonight. I have something I…" the waitress appeared bringing their second serving of wine and interrupting Piers' sentence.

"Will you be needing anything else before we seat you in the dining room?" she asked sweetly.

Helen noted his slight annoyance. He didn't use his usual charm with the woman when he answered.

"This will be all. We're waiting on our friend to arrive."

Helen waited for the waitress to leave and gave him a smile, "You were saying?

"Yes," he continued. His demeanor was stiffer than usual, as if he was trying to work out the right approach for something. "I want you to know that I've been thinking about…"

"Hi!" Martha said arriving at their table with a cheery grin. "Sorry I took so long. You were right, Helen, that tub is to kill for." Piers gave one last nervous glance at Helen and rose from his seat.

"Hello, Martha." He rose and gave her a hug pulling out her seat for her to sit. "Helen tells me you've been mucking about at Lord Percy Farthingay's massive old house."

"Yes, what a weirdo, the nephew, I mean," Martha said causing Piers to choke on his wine laughing out loud.

"You do have a way with words, Martha," he finally said wiping his chin with a napkin. "Why do you think he's a weirdo?"

"He reminds me of a nut job back in my hometown in Arkansas, except Brickstone is a lot more handsy."

She held her hands up and wiggled her fingers before putting a napkin daintily on her lap.

Piers studied Martha for a moment. "How old was he?"

"Well," Martha said slowly, "he wasn't a day over forty. Plenty old enough for acting like a wolf around Helen."

"Forty?" Piers said snippily.

Helen shook her head. "Oh, really, Martha. He didn't makeup to me. You're imagining things."

"He had that look in his eyes like you were a lamb chop and a dinner bell was being rung somewhere."

Martha signaled to the waitress.

Piers leaned back in his chair with an annoyed tightness to his expression.

"He was a bit odd, though," she continued. "The place was kept dark. He said he suffered from a sensitivity to natural light, though he had a tan and the moaning from Lord Percy kept under lock and key somewhere in that pile still gives me the shivers."

"What?" Piers exclaimed a trifle too loudly. People in the cocktail bar turned to look at the three of them.

"That's what he said, and the maid, Denise, told me it was Lord Percy who moaned because he didn't want to eat his gruel or something like that," Martha said sipping her fruity drink, her eyes darting surreptitiously back and forth between Helen and Piers.

"Helen, something is not right about this situation," Piers said firmly. "I don't think you should go back there again."

"Oh, not to worry, Piers," she answered. "The manuscript is being removed by armored vehicle and safely housed at an insurer in London. I'll be working with a slew of other experts in a clean, modern office building, with lots of regular people, not old, dark and damp manor houses with lascivious lords."

"Good word for him, Helen, lascivious," Martha added, with one eye on Piers' face. "That comment about steak tartare."

Martha rolled her eyes. "You know, I was thinking about today while I was soaking in the tub. It reminds me of something that happened to me as a young girl."

Not waiting for encouragement, Martha jumped into her story. She leaned in to talk more intimately with Helen and Piers.

"There was something predatory in Brickstone's nature. You have to be careful with those types. When I was about seventeen, there was this man who used to come into the Ben Franklin store where I worked. He had this floaty way about him even though he was a large man and he wore this necklace with only one big eye painted on a medallion. One day, he'd been breezing around the aisles taking his time picking things up and putting them back down when the only other customer in the store left. He made a beeline straight to me, but I saw him coming and got the counter between us. He towered over me and leaned across the checkout counter. I backed up close to the tall shelves behind me. In this slithering tone, he told me to look at his necklace hanging around his lumpy neck. I did what he asked because I was alone in the store, and I didn't want to antagonize him. I remember he leaned in closer and with garlic breath whispered, 'I'm a warlock and very powerful.'"

"What happened?" Helen and Piers said jointly, leaning in as Martha's voice dropped for effect.

"I know. It was creepy. I played dumb because I thought that was the best way to put him off the scent. So, I said to him in a sweet, upbeat way, 'That's neat, Mr. Chambers. I'll tell my dad. He was saying the other day he'd like to find someone who can help him clean all his guns'."

"What?" Piers asked, befuddled.

"Yeah, that was the exact expression of old weirdo Chambers. He stood there across the counter looking at me like I'd slapped him across the face. As he started to try to explain to me what a warlock was, the tiny bell over the front door tinkled, signaling that another customer was entering the store. He shuffled around the aisles a while longer and I saw that he was thinking hard about what I'd said. Finally, his intelligence caught up with his ego and he realized the significance of my last four words."

"Which were?" Helen asked, her eyebrows knitting.

"Clean all his guns," Martha replied, giggling at her own story.

Piers burst out laughing. "I bet he found his way out of the store without attempting to enlighten you further, Martha."

"The sad thing is how long it took him to put two and two together. He must not have been an effective warlock if he was that slow on the uptake."

The waitress appeared at their table and asked if they were ready to go into the dining room.

"I haven't seen Lord Percy since my days at Eton," Piers said as they stood to go into dinner. "He was an associate of my father's and they served on a banking board together. Come on, ladies, I'm famished."

"Me, too," Martha said. "Let's begin with a cheese plate."

CHAPTER 11

"Excuse me, Mr. Brickstone," Denise said, as she entered the room.

"Yes, Denise," he answered not taking his eyes off a magazine article about private islands for sale in the Caribbean.

"Miss Sutherland has been calling. She wishes for you to please come to your uncle's room."

Sighing, the heir of the manor put down his glossy magazine and stood up. Without a word to Denise, he walked out of the room. The Lord was housed on the opposite side of the house. It was quieter that way. Brickstone reflected on how the walk would be a good after dinner exercise.

This venture was proving to be extremely profitable and the manuscript he'd shown the two women today might buy him his own beautiful green island swimming in an azure sea. Selling off different valuables from the estate required time and patience, though. Getting through all the rooms would likely take another year. The library was a treasure trove.

As he walked, he considered his situation. It was surprising how tough Farthingay was, despite his eighty years. Even with the constant dosing of his food with sedatives, he still managed a good row once a week. The rants were getting tiresome, though, and it might have been wiser to get rid of him altogether.

"Not adding murder to a rap sheet, well not unless I have to," Brickstone mumbled to himself, as he took a quick look over his shoulder to make sure he was alone.

He'd chosen Melissa to manage the real owner of Greenwoods because controlling women, in Brickstone's opinion, was much easier than dealing with men. In his many years of work, he'd always found that his charm kept women from becoming long-term problems. If you found the right kind of simple female, she was putty in your hands. Sex, pretense at love and a few trinkets, kept them wanting to please you. Men, on the other hand, wanted their fair share.

Finally, he arrived at an area of the house not used in many long years. At one time, it must have been the quarters for the kitchen staff. His steps echoed in the empty corridor. At the far end of the hallway was a solid looking door and he heard a man's voice arguing with a woman's. Once there, he knocked and the voices ceased instantly.

A lock moved on the other side of the door, and soon a female face with eyes lined in black peeked around the edge.

"Melissa, it's me, Ricky," Brickstone whispered. "What's gotten into you?"

"You alone?" the woman softly said, trying to see around him and down the long, tight hallway.

"All alone, baby. Having a tough time with Lord Fartingay?"

"Ah, Ricky, that's real funny," Melissa said in a whiny voice beginning to grow more tremulous with each passing second. "It's getting to me, Ricky, keeping him in here all the time. I keep hearing things. How much longer have we got before we can leave this wretched, moldy place. I don't want to play nurse to this old goat any longer."

"Is that you, Brickstone?" a man's voice croaked from inside. "You can't hold me here much longer. My real nephew in Auckland visits in January and he'll want to see me. I'm not dead!"

"Not yet anyway! But that can be handled!" Ricky yelled roughly back.

Ricky turned his attention back to the young woman.

"Better find a way to keep him quiet, Melissa. This place is stuffed from floor to ceiling with priceless gems. It may take another six months or more to unload it all. Why don't you increase his medication? Keep him asleep until May for all I care."

"It's too dangerous, Ricky. It might kill him, he's so old," Melissa replied with a shiver of disgust. "I don't want him to die. I'd feel terrible."

"Well, it's up to you, baby. This place is a gold mine and I'm not leaving until every last farthing is squeezed from it."

Melissa slipped through the door and wrapped her arms around Ricky's neck. She squirmed up against him. "Can I buy anything I want? You promised me I could when we get this job done," she cooed.

"Anything," he said reaching down and giving her a slap on her backend. She giggled and shut the door between them and Lord Percy, tied to his bed.

"Denise said we had visitors today. Two women came. Were they pretty?" Melissa asked, her eyes searching his for truth in what he would say.

"No, baby," he lied, not flinching at his perjury. "Those two are going to sell something so valuable, I'm thinking about buying an island with the money from it."

Melissa squirmed and set a puckered pout to her mouth. "How will we keep the nephew from Auckland away?"

"I've been reading all Farthingay's emails. The nephew believes the old man is going to visit a friend in Hawaii and pretending to be Farthingay, I wrote telling him to visit next June instead. It's all taken care of, but don't tell him. Better to keep it quiet."

He gave her a deep kiss while running his hands up and down her back. Melissa softened and relaxed. Even while he kissed her, his mind was on Martha. Something about her wouldn't quit nagging at his brain. She definitely wasn't his type. It was the way she'd kept staring at him like he was dirty somehow. The comment about her being a paralegal swam up into his thoughts.

Like a bolt from the blue, it hit him. His mouth froze on Melissa's as the answer came to him.

"We might be in for some trouble," he said dropping Melissa like a dishrag.

"Why?" she practically cried, her lipstick smeared around her thin-lipped mouth.

"I remembered where I've seen one of those women who came today."

"Where?"

"Court. I saw her in court. She was working with one of the solicitors years ago when I was brought up on fraud charges after pulling that deal at the bank where I worked."

"Oh, God, Ricky!" Melissa exclaimed, "Do you think she recognized you?"

"Nah, I don't think so. We may need to wrap up our gig soon, baby," he said. "Might need to get out of here."

"Fantastic, I hate it here," she said, her eyes bright with hope.

Ricky was already half-way down the hall. "Better get back to work."

Melissa called after his retreating figure, "Come see me in the morning, right?"

"Get back to the old man, Melissa. Keep him quiet, but alive. We don't want any deaths on our hands." He heard her door close as he walked away. Under his breath and with a crook of a smile, he added, "Not yet, anyway."

CHAPTER 12

Johns was relieved to have some time to think over the Saundra situation before telling Martha. He knew she would be upset. Saundra had fought their divorce for so long and now he understood why. Legally, she had a right to half of what he owned, and, of course, she wanted it.

He'd awakened that morning aware of how alone he was and the real cost of Saundra's narcissism. His mother, Polly, was watching Martha's furry children at Flower Pot Cottage. The thought of Polly made him throw one arm over his eyes to block out the morning light from his bedroom window. Once she knew Saundra was back in town, it was likely she'd brew up a storm of her own. Polly hated Saundra with a passion. Both women had always gone at each other with everything in their arsenals. His thoughts were dispelled by his phone ringing on his bedside table.

"Johns," he answered.

The voice on the phone was bright and cheerful. "Good morning, Chief. It's Constable Waters speaking. We've got everything ready for a run through on the pies. What time do you want to start?"

Waters was one of the Chief's favorite constables. She worked hard, never complained and was a fantastic cook. He counted on her to stay calm and cool even when elbow-deep in difficult-to-make pie crust.

"Be there in about twenty minutes, Waters. Let's use the kitchen in the constabulary. Are Sam and Michael there yet?"

"Yes," Johns heard the exasperation in Water's voice. "Sam needs to be brought around to my way of thinking, so expect a sullen teenager when you get here."

"Tell him Celine Rupert is also in this Bake-Off. That should do the trick," Johns said, with a touch of humor.

"Oh, yes, that should brighten his cheerless self considerably."

Johns' phone made a beeping sound indicating another call was coming in. He quickly glanced at the screen and saw it was his solicitor.

"Hey, Waters, I need to take this incoming call. I'll be there soon."

He tapped 'end call' and 'accept'. "Hello, this is Merriam Johns."

"Good morning, Merriam, would you like the good news first or the expensive news," a gruff voice said on the other end of the line. Simon Graves, Johns' solicitor, and favorite fishing buddy, sounded like he was jogging on a treadmill.

"I'm ready, Simon. Hit me with the expensive news first."

"Saundra is asking for half of the farm's worth which her solicitor says is in the region of seven to seven and a half hundred thousand pounds."

Johns sat back down on the bed. The first wave of emotion was sheer disbelief at the amount she was asking for, the second wave of emotion was a slow-growing anger.

"Hope the next piece of information you've got for me Simon is good or you'd better send someone over here to the farm that knows how to use a defibrillator."

"Well," Simon said huffing for air while his feet thumped rapidly in rhythm with the hum of the exercise machine, "if you sell the farm, you won't get a million-five in this market, so they're throwing out a big number in hopes of settling for a much tighter one. I think we should low-ball them."

"This is the good news, right?" Johns asked. He wasn't sure what constituted positive and negative in Simon's legal world. "I don't want to sell my home and I don't want to give Saundra her blood money."

"I'd like to tell you, old Trout (Simon's nickname for Johns) there's a way to get out of paying her the money, but I can't see how. She's entitled, and you're going to be writing a check for around three to four hundred thousand, that is, if I do my job right."

"Simon, how long do I have?"

"Ten days, Trout. She's got a firm from London, real heavy hitters. Better talk with your mum and decide. I think you should put the farm up for sale. It'll buy you some time."

"Thanks, Simon. I'll call you tomorrow."

Johns tapped 'end' on his phone and laid it down beside him on the bed. Putting his head in his hands, he sat for a moment, trying to take in what it meant to lose the farm. Generations of his family had called it home. Polly, his mother, worked her brewing business out of one of the old dairy barns. Centuries of hard work raising cattle, generations of children's height marks on an oak post in the kitchen, and worn stone floors from hundreds of feet treading throughout the old house were all testimonies to the number of Johnses who'd called the farm their home.

Looking out between his fingers, his gaze fell on the floor. He'd have to tell Polly today, no way around it. The idea of her having to leave her home made him heartsick. Getting up, he turned on the hot water in his shower. First things first. He needed to get to town and make a pie.

Scene break

After a deliciously decadent sleep, Helen was already up and dressed. She and Piers were going Christmas shopping. He'd promised to take her into the nearby village where she could pick out gifts for everyone on her list. What was promising, she thought to herself, was that Piers seemed as excited as she was about spending the day browsing through quaint shops.

"Helen!" It was Martha clambering to be let in through the adjoining door.

"Hey, what's up?" Helen asked, swinging the door open to reveal a flannel-robed Martha.

"Would it be a problem to head home late this afternoon?" Martha asked.

"No, that's fine. We could leave after Piers and I get back from shopping. Around three o'clock?"

"Thanks, Helen. Polly sent me a text with her thoughts on the first round of competition. I want to do a few practice runs and if we get home tonight, Polly and I can work on it."

"Sure, am I also doing a pie in the first round?"

"No, you're on for puddings, but we all have to work on the tea section which is the second day's competition." Martha gave Helen a good look up and down. "You're stunning, Helen. I like your sweater--very pretty."

"Thanks," Helen replied. "What are you up to this morning?"

"I'm going to get a massage, a pedicure and a facial today. I'll catch up with you about two-thirty."

"I'll be ready to go. Enjoy yourself."

"I will."

The door shut behind Martha, and Helen grabbed her purse and headed downstairs. At the reception area, waited Piers. He was wearing comfortable walking boots, a mid-length coat and a festive red muffler. Upon seeing Helen, he gave her a bright smile.

"Are you ready, m'lady?" he said reaching for her hands.

She offered both of hers to his and, like two people who are in love, their gaze locked for a brief moment. She blushed like a young girl and he leaned in to kiss her but remembered they were in a public place, so only brushed his lips against her warm cheek.

"Come on, I've got a treat for you," he said, his excitement showing in his voice. "I'm glad you dressed well. It's not far to the village, but it did snow last night, so…"

He opened the front door of the hotel and there in the courtyard waited the most enchanting two-man sleigh that Helen had ever seen. Painted green with gold trimming, it looked like something out of a fairytale. An elegant bay mare waited patiently at its front.

"How wonderful, Piers!" Helen exclaimed. "I love it! It is a treat indeed."

He helped her in and covered her with fur robes and quilts to keep her warm. Settling himself, he took the reins and gave the horse the signal to trot. People smiled and waved as they pulled away from the courtyard. Helen snuggled up close to Piers and they didn't speak a word between them. They didn't need to. Their thoughts were on each other as the sleigh glided like a dream into a winter wonderland of a snowy Yorkshire countryside.

CHAPTER 13

"What the Hell are you saying, Merriam?" Polly practically growled. "That woman is in this village? And a judge?"

"Yes," Chief Johns said briefly. His mother was only slightly over five feet tall, but she packed a wallop when she wanted to.

"I won't participate. It would be a farce for me to do so. She'll never give my team a fair chance," Polly said, banging the large lump of pie crust dough down on a breadboard.

"Mum, it's more than that."

Chief Johns had deliberately picked this moment to talk with his mother. He'd already been to the Constabulary and worked with his team on their pies and menus for the competition. Afterwards, he headed over to Martha's cottage where his mother was trying to perfect her pie crust recipe.

Polly's hands were wrapped around a rolling pin like she was trying to throttle it.

"What? There's more?" she said, smacking the wooden pin against her palm. "I don't know what you ever saw in that woman, other than the obvious."

"Mum, put the rolling pin down and please have a seat. Do you have some tea to drink?" He searched the diminutive kitchen for signs of tea.

Polly's eyes narrowed. She plopped into one of the table's Windsor wooden chairs.

"I give up," she said, slumping down deep into a limp position. "Tell me what you've come here to say."

He sat there, trying to summon the nerve to tell his mother she was about to lose the only home she'd ever loved. Taking a deep, stabilizing breath, he said the worst thing he could think to say to her.

"Saundra won't give me the divorce unless I sell the farm or give her half of what it's worth."

There was only silence in Martha's homey kitchen where two humans and three small animals sat. Polly didn't speak. She didn't yell. All she did was look out the curtained window over the sink and watch the snowflakes drift by. Johns sat with his hands folded in his lap waiting for what he expected to be the inevitable tirade, denouncing Saundra for what she was, an evil, greedy she-devil.

"Will it be the end of her?" his mother finally asked without any emotion in her voice.

"Yes."

"So be it, Merriam. Sell it." Polly's demeanor was perfectly peaceful and without malice of any kind. "If it sets you free, it's worth giving her every farthing we've got. It's not too late for you, sweetheart, to have a life with someone who loves you. You need to talk with Martha about this soon."

"I will. I will. I want to have proof I've been working on this divorce. It's important."

Polly got up, dusted the flour from her apron and gave Merriam a loving smile.

"Come on, child. Get going. Go talk with that solicitor of yours and call on Mr. Crabtree who deals with property. I've got my eye on a more manageable place here in the village anyway. I want to be closer. Feels safer."

Merriam was in shock. He sat in his chair like a lump of clay. Polly took up her rolling pin and worked the dough.

"Mum, are you okay?" he asked softly.

She walked over to her son and cupped his face in her hands.

"Nothing matters to me, Merriam, but you. Things are worthless compared to someone you love." She looked deep into his eyes, searching them. "If you know you are free, dear, let me see it in your eyes."

She pulled his head to her breast and as she did so, his entire being suddenly realized what it meant to be truly free from all the pain, loneliness, and bitterness he'd known for years. He was truly free. If this was Saundra's price, it would be paid. It was cheap compared to the release it bought for his soul.

Tears welled up in his stinging eyes and he let Polly hold him like she'd done when he was a child and scared of the dark or sick with the flu. They were both free from Saundra. It was the most peace either of them had known in a long, long time.

Scene Break

Martha sat patiently in the hotel reception area waiting for Helen. The Mercedes had been brought around by the steward, and Martha's things were already in the trunk. When she'd seen Helen earlier, her friend's whole demeanor was brighter, happier than Martha had ever known it to be since she'd known her. It was nice to see Helen this way.

"I'm here!" Helen called from the stair landing as she descended with her bags. "Sorry, it took so long. Piers forgot his keys were in my pocket. I ran them back up to him."

The opportunity was too perfect. Martha gave into it and teased Helen.

"Seems awful friendly, his keys, your pocket. What *have* you two been up to today?"

Helen stopped dead in the reception area, her bags swinging from each shoulder. The expression on her face as she quickly scanned the intimate area for anyone who might have heard Martha's insinuation was that of a prim person startled by a secret truth.

"Shhhh," she instructed Martha, who was smiling like a Cheshire cat. "I'll tell you in the car."

Martha could hardly wait. In an effort to hurry, she picked up Helen's Louis Vuitton bag and handed the steward a tip as a thank you for bringing the car around. With Helen in tow, Martha threw the bags in the car's back seat and settled herself in the passenger seat.

"Come on, Juliet!" she called to Helen, who was still fiddling with her purse.

Helen rolled her eyes heavenward and with what composure she was able to manage after being hustled out of one of Warwickshire's better hostelries, she opened the driver's-side door and sat down.

"Whew! That was like herding chickens," Martha said.

Helen turned on the car engine. "I'm going to hurt you."

"Why? Let's roll and you can tell me all about your date with Piers today." Martha's smile was open and friendly, like a cheerful Labrador, who wants to play ball. "I know something's up because you have a certain sparkle going on," Martha massaged the air around Helen's head, "in this whole area."

"Stop fussing with my…space," Helen grumped. "Give me a minute to find the right road. The snow is thick and I need to concentrate."

The Mercedes lurched out through the two tall stone pillars designating the entrance to the Brentmore Hotel. Helen increased the speed of the sedan and sighed.

"We're off and I can tell you everything, now."

"Spill it," Martha quipped.

"It was sheer bliss. He took me for a ride in a sleigh pulled by a sweet tempered mare all the way into the nearby village of Stratford. We shopped and he had everything wrapped and sent to Healy for me to pick up later."

"What a sweetheart!" Martha cooed. "I'm beginning to like that man more every day. Better grab him, Helen, before I throw my hat into the ring."

Helen reached over and pinched Martha on the arm.

"Listen here, Red, you better be teasing."

Martha laughed and rubbed the spot of the playful pinch. "It's fun to see how much you actually like him, Helen. By the way, I'm hungry. Want to stop along the way and have a nice cup of warm soup somewhere?"

"Nope. We're getting home. The roads will be terrible until we reach the highway and I've still got to organize some things with Sinead Peters in London. I want to put this Brickstone project behind us, Martha. Piers thinks it's not on the up and up."

"I agree. Let's get Merriam involved. Back to your shopping-trip story, Helen. Was it romantic?" Martha asked wistfully.

"It was *so* romantic. He was a perfect gentleman the entire day." After a short pause, she added, "I am scared, Martha."

"Why?"

"I love him."

"Oh, boy, Helen. Those are big words to be throwing around only one year after Georgie Porgie left town."

"I know, but to be fair, loser George never, never came close to being anything like Piers. Give me some credit. Piers is steak to George's hamburger."

Martha had never met George, but she'd seen pictures. Helen was stating a simple truth with that last comment.

"Yeah, and he better be playing for keeps, or I'm going to let him have it," Martha said. She didn't want Helen to be hurt again, and Piers held too many of the cards.

"Don't give him your body, Helen. That's all I've got to say. He's used to getting everything he sets his mind to, and he's got to learn you're worth more than a few fun romps in the hay." Vehement in her tone, Martha eyed Helen, who sat elegantly composed in her seat holding the wheel with both hands.

For a few seconds, she didn't answer but sat watching as the road unfurled ahead of them. In a soft voice, she said, "It's hard to stay sure and strong sometimes, Martha. I was so lost when George ran off with Fiona, a girl practically half my age. I don't trust Piers. How can I? How can I ever trust any man again after that?"

Martha sat mute in her seat. The truth was she didn't trust Cousins either, but she didn't want Helen to lose faith in the future. Martha would have to toss Cousins into the river in front of his precious Healy House if she found out he was only playing Helen. For the time being, though, she needed to shore up Helen's faith in the male side of humanity.

"Has he tried to get you in bed, Helen?"

"Well," she hem hawed, "he's been pretty ardent, but I feel so insecure about the whole thing, so I've not let it go too far."

"Good. Wait till you're certain of your own feeling."

"Really? It's getting harder and harder each time, Martha."

"So be it. Keep your head together, Helen, until you know for sure you're ready to accept either consequence."

"Which is?"

"One, he loves you and wants to make you his only. That means he doesn't want to lose you. He wants something more traditional. The second option is you're ready for the free love, free milk scenario."

"Yes, to the first one. That's more me. I'm the type, if I'm honest with myself, who wouldn't be happy keeping it loose and free."

Martha continued. "There's no value put on something that comes too easily. It's a lost truth these days, but it still holds water. Piers knows that, as well. He sees something special in you. Something he's not likely to see again in this life and he knows it."

CHAPTER 14

"Hell is empty and all the devils are here."

-Shakespeare, The Tempest, Act I, Scene II

It was the next morning and the official beginning of the Marsden-Lacey Pudding and Pie Bake-Off. They were kicking off the event with a Meet and Greet. Martha, Polly, and Helen had decided on their recipes the previous evening after the girls got home to Flower Pot Cottage. Mr. O'Grady, Polly's beau and fourth team member, was happy to be along for the ride. They were ready to take on the other teams.

All the contestants and the judges were under one roof to discuss the rules of competition and to talk with the local press, who'd come to Marsden-Lacey for the scoop on the Pudding and Pie Bake-Off. Helen and Martha were doing some walking about to check out the competition.

"Did you see that woman who is hanging on Johns, Martha?" Helen said nudging Martha in the ribs and pointing across the room to the place where a stage was erected.

Martha craned her head to see over the multitude of competitors, visitors, and press. Sure enough, Merriam's tie was being fiddled with by a petite woman. Martha scowled.

"Who is she? I've not seen her in Marsden-Lacey before."

Helen, with a critical eye for female deportment, answered, "Well, she's a bit of a tart, if you ask me. She's got too much makeup on. I can see it from across the hall."

Martha giggled lightly. "Let's stroll over there and get a better look at *all* the competition, if you know what I mean. Shall we?"

The girls worked their way across an extremely crowded and hot room. People were excited to see friends, some of the contestants were talking with a television crew from Leeds and a few local dignitaries were busy having their pictures taken by the Marsden-Lacey Times.

A sharp buzzing sound blared from above and a voice, they both well knew, blasted much too sharply from the overhead speakers, causing everyone to slap their hands over their ears.

"Hello! Hello! Am I able to be heard?" Señor Agosto, Piers Cousin's high-tempered Spanish chef at Healy House, said into the microphone.

"Ah, yes, it is working nicely. Everyone, may I have your attention, please," he said. "I would like to introduce to you our judging team for our first annual Marsden-Lacey Pudding and Pie Bake-Off."

A huge round of applause filled the Village Hall's auditorium. Helen and Martha's progress was checked by the crowd's sudden push as everyone tried to get closer to the stage.

Martha saw the woman who'd been playing up to Merriam. She was taking her place alongside Alistair Turner, Lana Chason and, of course, Señor Agosto.

"She must be a judge," Martha whispered to Helen, who was trying not to rub up against anyone. Look, there's Lana.

One of the caterers came by with a tray of drinks. He offered one to Martha, but she declined with a polite, "No thank you."

"Does it feel hot to you in here?" Helen asked Martha.

"Yes, it's miserable." Martha quickly checked out Helen's face. She could see how white Helen was. "Oh, did mentioning Lana make you upset? I'm sorry, kid. You look pale, Helen. Go over to the seats by that cracked window and get some fresh air."

Helen nodded and extricated herself from the pressed bodies of the crowd. Señor Agosto resumed his introductions.

"If you will please come forward as I introduce your name, judges. I'll give a short biography of your expertise." Two ladies beside Martha whispered about the lanky American blonde, whom Martha knew was Lana. They were questioning her expertise, since she looked like a supermodel. Martha raised her eyebrows at the comment. It was a good question, but she knew better than to assume anything about a person's abilities by looking at their cover.

"Mrs. Lana Chason Berkowitz comes to us from New Orleans, Louisiana," Agosto said. Martha's face broke out into a huge smile. She turned to find Helen in the place she'd told her to sit. Helen's eyes were shut, and she was still pale, but there was no mistaking the large grin on her face. Lana was remarried and off the market.

Agosto rambled on about her time spent at a famous cooking school in California as a teacher and her time spent writing a column for a well-known Southern magazine. He turned to the dapper Alistair Turner, everyone's favorite ex-con or ex-spy, no one knew which.

"Our Mr. Turner, has a diploma from Le Cordon Bleu in Paris for Bakery. He worked as head Chef for the three-star restaurant, Sylvie's, on Montserrat, and recently finished his first book, to be published in May, called *Breaking Bread: A Guide to Baking and Dining With Friends*."

"Those two never cease to surprise me with what they do, who they know, and where they've been," Merriam Johns said in Martha's ear. His voice was so close, she jumped and turned around.

"Hey! You startled me. Who's the blonde floozie fiddling with your tie?" she countered, ignoring his comment regarding Perigrine and Alistair.

Johns gave her a serious look. "That's something I need to talk to you about. Would you come with me outside for a moment?"

Before she was able to answer him, she heard Agosto say, "And also with us, is a Manchester native and famous chef in her own right, Saundra Johns, wife of our own Chief Constable, Merriam Johns."

The look on Merriam's face told Martha everything. Her heart froze in her chest. She couldn't believe it. Her brain simply shut down.

"Tell me it isn't what it sounds like," she said, searching his face.

He reached for her. With both of his hands, he cupped her face. "Martha, she's my wife, but I don't love her. We've been separated for over five years. I've been trying to get a divorce for the last two, since I met you. I've been putting pressure on her for the last six months. You've got to let me explain everything to you."

Martha reached up and took hold of his wrists and pulled them downward. Shaking her head from left to right in disbelief, she said in a voice she didn't recognize, "No, I don't want to talk right now. You need to go away. I can't look at you. Where's Helen?"

Johns stood stalk still towering over the pretty redhead who only came up to his shoulder. Martha couldn't feel anything but her face flushing and herself becoming overheated. She turned on Johns and wandered off through the crowd until she saw Helen still lying her head against the window, with her eyes shut.

Martha plopped down beside her. She, too, laid her head against the cool windowpane and let the outside air, chilled from the winter weather, filter across her burning brow.

"Johns is married," she croaked.

Helen sat up straight in her chair, her face white and her hair damp from snow coming in through the window's crack. Sprigs of frozen hair were sticking straight out giving Helen the look of a lopsided ice queen or drunk punk rocker from the eighties.

The vision made Martha chuckle, despite the news she'd learned.

"Are you hysterical?" Helen asked, looking more perplexed and porcupine-like than before.

"No, no, I'm can't help it. Your hair is all pointy and frozen with a bunch of snow sprinkles. Oh! My God! Helen, Johns is married! I'm you!" Martha cried, the reality of the situation hitting her once more.

Helen's frozen hair quivered as she wrestled herself into a better position to see Martha's face straight on.

"You're me? What the hell are you talking about? Do I need to get you medical attention?" she asked, her color cool, but her tone hot.

"Merriam is someone I can't trust. Don't you see? He's like Georgie Porgie, your ex-husband, a total jerk."

Helen's face slowly registered understanding, and she nodded up and down. Returning to her earlier position with her head against the cold window, she finally said in a queasy voice, "Yes, that's me, all right."

For a minute, they sat unmoving until Helen reached over and patted Martha on the leg in a reassuring, motherly way.

"Does this remind you of anything?" she asked.

Martha, with her eyes shut and in the same position as Helen, said, "Oh you betcha it does, except this time there's no body on the floor."

"Give it time. Give it time," Helen murmured.

"God, I hope not."

"I only meant that with our luck, it may happen," Helen added.

Martha opened her eyes and gave Helen a good look.

"Hey, should I take you home? Did something make you sick over there in the crowd? Lana's married. She's no longer a threat."

"I know. I know. It's that I haven't eaten enough I think, and the room was so hot with all the people crowding together. It was a bit of a shock to see Lana, but I'm feeling ill and I want to get out of here."

"Stay put. I'm going to grab you something to eat and you're going to eat all of it, Skinny Butt," Martha said. She stood up and found the long table with plates of sandwiches, fruit salad, and hot tea. Putting a few things on a plate and making two cups of tea with milk and honey, she went back to where Helen was sitting.

"Here," she said putting a napkin over Helen's lap. "Eat!"

The girls sat and munched on fresh fruit, a slice of ham on a croissant with cheese and a couple of goat cheese samosas. Soon, Helen said she was feeling better.

"Here comes Merriam, Martha. He looks like a beat cat. Better give him a chance to explain. You don't want to assume you know his situation. Take a deep breath and hear him out," she advised.

Johns approached hesitantly.

"Martha would you please give me a few minutes to talk with you?"

"One condition, Merriam," she said, her hand in a stop guard position.

"Name it," he said.

"Please go find, Piers. He needs to come over and take Helen home. She's not well. The heat has been too overwhelming."

Johns nodded and threaded back through the crowd. Soon, he arrived with Piers, who looked worried and picked Helen up and carried her out of the building with her protesting the entire time. Martha laughed and waved. Turning to Johns, she said, "I'd like to take a wooden spoon to you like my mother did when I lied as a child. It taught me to respect her and the truth. Lying in the end, is more painful for everyone involved."

"I know, I know, Martha. It's a long story."

"I don't have time to discuss this at the moment, Merriam. I'm not sure I want to talk with you until you can give me a pretty damn good reason for not telling me. The press is taking each team's photo and Polly told me to be ready. We can discuss it when I've cooled down. I'll see you later."

Martha found her way back through the bustle of humanity, and seeing Polly, she told her that Helen was not feeling well and wouldn't be able to be photographed.

"Have you met my daughter-in-law, the judge, yet," Polly asked, giving Martha a mug with a dry tea bag in it.

"No, and why didn't you mention this last night or EVER? What's the tea for?" Martha asked.

"Not my place to discuss it with you before Merriam did. I've asked him multiple times if he'd told you yet. I think he didn't want to ever talk about Saundra. How about we have a nice chat about the whole thing before they interview us and take our picture?"

"Okay," Martha said with a heavy sigh. A twinge of regret at not giving Merriam a chance to explain pulled at her heart. "I have the feeling you have something to get off your chest, Polly. Where's the hot water?"

"Down at the end of the table. I'll go with you."

Polly and Martha didn't have to wait long. One of the men helping at the hot water dispenser offered to take their mugs and fill them.

But as he took their cups, a female voice came from behind Martha. "Are you going to introduce us, Mother Johns?"

Martha, still facing Polly, took her thumb and pointed it at her own sternum in the direction of the voice coming from directly behind her. She mouthed the words 'Is that her?'

Polly nodded up and down with a sour look on her face. Turning around, Martha offered her hand to Saundra, who declined to accept it.

"I'm Martha Littleword," Martha said, putting her hand down.

"And I'm Saundra, Merriam's wife. Been dating him long?"

"Who?" Martha said, playing coy.

Saundra blinked. "Why Merriam, my husband, of course," she said sardonically, while handing the man at the hot water dispenser her mug to fill as well. "He's been watching you since you arrived, so I guessed you must be the local flavor of the month."

Martha laughed derisively. "How sweet you are to be so interested in me, a complete and total stranger."

Polly chuckled and sipped her tea.

"Well, I am a judge for the competition. I should take an interest in the competitors. You look like you know a thing or two about...cooking," Saundra quipped with one eyebrow arched. She looked Martha up and down. "It must be the big American appetite in you. Lots of experience with food," Saundra sneered.

"Yes, thank you," Martha returned in a nonplused, regal way. With a slow turn of her waist so that Saundra would be forced to apprehend Martha's buxom chest area, she said, "We are a fortunate people, so well endowed with plentiful resources."

Martha picked up one of the mugs filled from the attendant and gave Saundra an indifferent smile. Turning again to the table, she picked up another mug and handed it to her.

"I was certain Merriam must be depressed," Saundra said, holding her tea mug, too, and blowing lightly across its brim to cool the hot liquid within. "He's been so lost without me. He's begged for so long for me to take him back."

"Really? I haven't seen him so happy in years as he's been the last six months," Polly piped in.

"Oh, Mother Johns. He appears to have given up. He wasn't into women who were...beefy before." Saundra's eyes glittered as she sipped her tea.

"Why you piece of..." Polly said, but Martha laughed heartily and held up her hand.

"Maybe it's not that he likes them beefy," she gave Saundra a quick appraisal, "but that he likes them to look like a woman."

Saundra's face turned beet-red. Martha thought the sling had hit home, so she smiled. Saundra coughed.

"Well, if we're done throwing dirt here," Martha said, "I think I'll find the camera crew." But Saundra's body went rigid. She lunged for Martha, who was taken off guard by the attack. Saundra's eyes widened with fear and she clung to Martha's sweater.

"I...I...I," she gurgled.

Martha held on to her, but the woman slipped from her grip down onto her knees. Polly tried to grab Saundra as well, but even with both their efforts, Saundra jerked free and gripped her throat.

"What's wrong with her?" Martha said, confused. "Is there a doctor? Anyone, is there a doctor here?"

Saundra lay on the floor jerking and convulsing. Saliva gurgled from her mouth. The people closest to them turned and yelled for a doctor, too. Aware of an emergency, the entire crowd pressed in on the three women. Martha knelt down over Saundra trying to lift her head to see what she was choking on.

One last convulsion, and Saundra Johns lay still, her eyes staring toward the ceiling. Beside her, lay her tea mug dashed to pieces. The entire crisis had taken less than a minute in total time.

"Saundra! Saundra!" Martha cried, shaking the woman by the shoulders. "What's wrong?"

"Oh, Martha! Stop. Stop shaking her. She's dead," Polly moaned from above.

People talked loudly and called for an ambulance. Like a bolt from the blue, Martha realized it was her dream. It was coming to life all around her. She let go of Saundra and sat back on her heels, shaking her head. With great effort, Martha tried to grab onto pieces of reality, but her vision faded. Voices became muffled. The last thing she heard was a woman's voice saying, "She's fainted. Martha's fainted."

CHAPTER 15

"Dead? Santa Maria! Why?" Señor Agosto's chef's hat was askew and slipping with each frantic twist of his head as he surveyed first the retreating crowd and the incoming emergency team.

"It must have been a heart attack. We're waiting for the ambulance to arrive. Chief Johns is with the body," Alistair Turner said standing by Agosto and watching spectators being turned out of doors by the police.

"Holy Mother of God," Agosto said, crossing himself as any good Catholic would in such a moment. "How can we make the puddings or the pies with such a catastrophe, a death so horrible?"

Alistair drew air into his lungs in a slow, thoughtful way and let it out. "We don't, not for today, anyway. I'd better talk with Chief Johns. He's got to be in a state of shock."

Agosto turned his head at an angle toward Alistair and gave him a knowing look.

"What?" Alistair asked.

"They were in a divorce. Did you not know? She had another lover," Agosto said plainly.

Alistair nodded as if convinced of the statement's veracity. "No, I didn't know. I've only been here a couple of years. Johns didn't look delighted when he heard she was coming to judge the contest."

"From my brief association with Mrs. Johns," Agosto said, slightly under his breath so only Alistair heard, "I quickly learned she was a formidable woman. Her manner was often... difficult."

"Here comes Johns."

Alistair and Agosto waited respectfully until the Chief made his way over to them.

"We're sorry Chief for this terrible thing," Agosto said gently. "Do you know how she died?"

Johns' expression was unreadable, but he shook his head saying, "We don't know anything yet. Saundra was a healthy woman. The body will be removed once forensics has their work done."

Piers came up to the group of men. He put his hand on the Chief's shoulder in a gesture of sympathy.

"I'm so sorry, Merriam. I didn't even know she was your wife."

"Thank you, but *'was'* is the operative word. Saundra *was* my wife, in name only. I've been suing for a divorce for a couple of years. We haven't lived together in over five. She wouldn't give me the divorce. Come to find out, she'd been waiting until she was certain of a few minor financial details."

All three of the other men nodded their heads in common understanding and sympathy of the Chief's true meaning.

"Difficult situation," Alistair said sagely.

"Ah, the female," Agosto said, in a tone of pure gravity, "they'll go to any lengths to procure their security."

"Indeed," Johns agreed.

The Chief looked miserable, irritated and pale. No one made a further comment. A young, efficient constable approached the static group of morose looking men.

"Sir, the body is on its way to Leeds. Dr. Townsend, the Head of forensics wants you to call her," the constable said gently.

Johns nodded and with a terse one-finger wave, indicated a goodbye of sorts to the sympathetic body of men. He disappeared through the Village Hall's front entrance.

Piers turned to Agosto and Alistair. "The school's gymnasium is the new venue for the Pudding and Pie Bake-Off. There isn't another building large enough and with the proper kitchen space. The Headmistress was more than willing to help us. It's her students we're trying to raise funds for and she wants to be a judge."

Agosto's posture became more upright. "Has she any qualifications?" he asked primly.

"She has an indoor area capable of holding, at least, five hundred people and a commercial kitchen with three cooking stoves," Piers said in a flat, pragmatic tone, "and she's not asking for us to pay for the electricity out of our proceeds."

"Sounds like she's perfect," Alistair put in.

"I agree," Agosto said, nodding, "perfect in every way."

Scene Break

Polly and Martha were sitting together in the Village Hall's secretary's office. The entire building was a crime scene, and for the last two hours, investigators had cordoned off sections with yellow tape, taken photographs, accumulated minute elements of evidence, and squeezed every last bit of information from witnesses.

Martha sighed. "I'm tired."

Polly got up and went over to the window. The sun was setting. "They've already taken our statements. It shouldn't be much longer."

"Tell me why no one has ever mentioned or hinted at the fact that Merriam was married?" Martha said, out of the blue.

Polly continued to stare out the window. "Merriam grew up here, Martha. It was well known what he endured during his marriage to Saundra. When she left him five years ago, we all breathed a sigh of relief. It was like a death, but one for which you feel grateful, once it finally arrives."

Martha watched the older woman's back. Being a mother herself, she was easily able to imagine Polly's pain at her son's situation.

"No one said anything to you because most of them believed he was divorced already. This horrible death will reopen all the wounds again, make people talk and ask questions. They'll learn he wasn't divorced, how she wouldn't give him one, how she had other lovers, and being human, they'll begin to whisper to each other about him, about how he was a cuckold and how, most likely, you're an American tart he took up with for easy sex."

Polly turned around. The look on her face broke Martha's heart. Getting up from where she'd been sitting, Martha walked over to Polly and wrapped her arms around her, giving her a warm, loving hug.

"American tart, huh?" Martha said, with a low chuckle.

"I was being nice, dear. It's probably more like a piece of tail, or something crude," Polly said, beginning to chuckle a bit, too. The two women went back to the settee and sat down again.

"As for the easy sex comment, why does everyone believe American women are so sleazy?" Martha asked.

"Wishful thinking on the men's part and worrying on the women's," Polly answered simply.

They sat quietly for a few minutes.

"I'm sorry, Polly. I can't imagine the pain you and Merriam went through."

"It was heartbreaking, Martha. He wanted children. We missed out on so, so much."

A woman pushed the office door open, startling Polly and Martha. They stood up quickly.

"Ladies, we only need your fingerprints. You'll be able to leave afterwards. Thank you for your patience," the officer said, while opening the door for them.

"Come on, Polly," Martha said, crooking her arm for Polly to slip hers through. As they walked out into the main room, their eyes both went to the spot where Saundra had died. Martha knew it would be a good time to say something distracting.

"I wouldn't make a good tart, Polly."

"I know," Johns' mother said firmly, her eyes averted from the place, "and that's why he was so worried to tell you. He'd lost so much already. He didn't want to lose you, too."

CHAPTER 16

"Cyanide killed her and a lot of it, Chief Johns. I'm so sorry."

The news from Dr. Jane Townsend, the Head of Forensics for the Criminal Investigation Department in Leeds, made Johns' legs go weak. A wave of nausea overcame him. He'd loved Saundra once, even passionately. He'd never wanted her to suffer.

With an effort to sound like he had some semblance of control, Johns steadied himself and answered.

"Thank you, Jinks. I have to let you go. I'll call you back in a few."

He put the phone down and a feeling he'd never experienced before, and would never again, welled up in him. Horror and relief vied with each other, followed by a twist of guilt. If he pushed back at either of the first two emotions, his mind quickly filled the void with something he should be doing or another image of Saundra.

"Got a moment?" Constable Waters stood at the door of his office, holding two cups of steaming tea.

"Come in," he mumbled, picking up a pen from his desk and beginning to scribble on a piece of paper.

Donna shut the door and sat down in a worn-out leather side chair. She pushed one of the cups over toward him. He stared at it like it was the first of its kind ever to be put in front of him.

"Go ahead," she said gently, "take it. It won't bite you and you need it."

When he looked up at her, his expression of absolute shock and confusion would have shaken anyone, At some point in anyone's life, they see that face on someone they love or they care for deeply.

Donna waited, sipping her tea. When he was ready, he would talk.

"Someone killed my wife, Donna," he said simply. "She was a selfish woman who lacked empathy of any kind. I loved her, once. They'll send another inspector, of course, from Leeds to handle the murder investigation. The contest is going to continue, but not until Friday. I won't be on our team, Waters. So, we need to find a replacement."

Johns picked up his tea mug, holding it in the palms of his hands. The heat emanating from its heavy, clay structure must have been a comfort.

Donna continued to drink her tea. She'd grown accustomed to murder. "We'll do our best, sir. Is there anything you need?"

"I need an alibi, for starters, but I don't have one. I was in the crowd at the Village Hall when she was murdered. So many people were there. Anyone could have slipped something into her drink."

"We have statements from over one hundred people as of eight o'clock this evening, Chief, that's about halfway through the crowd. The only people near your wife before she died were Mrs. Littleword and your mother, Mrs. Johns. The people at the refreshment table have all stated they didn't pay much attention to who stayed to chat around the table, once they'd received their food and drinks."

Johns sat for a moment, thinking. "Did you get statements from everyone who worked the refreshment table?"

"Not all," Donna replied.

"I want to see all the video footage from the television cameras. Get on that for me, Waters. I want it by nine o'clock tomorrow. Also, bring me the statements from the people who worked the refreshment table. The inspector from Leeds will be here sometime in the morning. I want to have a chance to go over everything first."

"You going to be okay, Sir?" Donna said, rising and walking to the door of his office. She was heading home for the evening.

"Work, Waters. Work does it every time."

Scene Break

It was nice to be in Martha's quiet, cozy living room. Piers had made a roaring fire before he left. Amos, Vera, and Gus were curled up by either Helen or Martha. Each woman was wrapped up in her favorite snuggly blanket. Martha's was made of fleece with a red and brown tartan design, while Helen's was an ample faux sheep's wool coverlet with enough breadth to encircle her at least twice.

Both girls sat gazing at the fire. Neither one wanted to leave the other. The last five hours had been extremely exhausting and after they'd finally sat down, they'd discussed, in detail, the saga of Johns, his wife and how Martha should proceed.

"I don't want to talk about it anymore," Martha was saying. "I'll talk with him when I'm ready. I've been thinking about your prediction."

"About what? I don't remember making a prediction," Helen said vaguely.

"We were sitting together, at the window in the Village Hall, and you said to give it time, with our luck there'd be another body on the floor."

Helen, mesmerized by the fire, nodded and roused herself. She slapped her forehead with the palm of her hand.

"That's terrible! I should be whipped for being so callous about something like that."

Helen heaved herself out of her chair and went down the hall to the kitchen. She continued talking as she went. "I said what I said in the Hall because I was feeling icky and the situation reminded me of our first meeting at The Grange. Besides, there's no magical mumbo jumbo making things happen because we say a few words."

Clanking sounds came from a saucepan being put on the stovetop. "Want more hot chocolate?" she called.

"What about 'Ask and ye shall receive'!" Martha yelled over the pan rattling and refrigerator scrounging sounds coming from the kitchen.

"That's different," came Helen's reply.

"How so? What we give voice to has a way of becoming reality. Don't you ever watch those great documentaries? I just finished one on quantum reality."

Helen shuffled back into the living room and pointed to Martha's mug, which was held it up for a refill of hot cocoa.

"If you're trying to insinuate Saundra's death has something to do with my comment in the Village Hall, you're nuts."

Helen folded herself up into the comfortable chair across from Martha.

"I think I am nuts," Martha mumbled.

She rubbed Gus' fur and scratched his ears, which kicked-off a low, contented purring emanating from his chest. "I'm trying to make sense out of the whole thing. Saundra's dying was almost exactly like my dream."

"Pure coincidence," Helen said, stirring her coco.

"Perhaps."

"That's neither here nor there, Martha, and you know you can't pin what happened with Saundra on something so esoteric. What *is* real, and I think you know it, too, is that Saundra Johns didn't die of a heart attack. I saw the woman and she was fit. Unless it was a massive stroke, she died of unnatural causes."

Martha was quiet for a moment. She nodded her head.

"I agree. When I was bending over her, she was gasping for breath and clutching her throat. I think it was poison."

Neither Helen or Martha said anything.

"Murdered," Helen said softly.

"Uh huh, it would have to be someone who had access to either something she ate or something she drank."

They both looked at each other in a way that suggested they didn't like what they were thinking.

"Johns would never have hurt his wife, but someone did," Helen said slowly, giving each word emphasis. "I hope to God, it wasn't Polly."

Martha's mouth was a hard, grim line as she sat staring into the crackling fire. She got up to head upstairs to bed. "Oh, Helen, I hope so, too. A mother will go to any lengths sometimes to save her child, even when he's twice her size and has twice her strength."

"It doesn't take much strength to poison, Martha."

"No," Martha agreed. "Poison is a woman's weapon. No doubt about it."

CHAPTER 17

Thursday, and it was supposed to be the first day of competition for the Pudding and Pie Bake-Off. Instead, they would resume the following day which was a Friday. Helen was working on her laptop and making phone calls. She'd heard back from Sinead Peters about the shipment of the manuscripts from Lord Percy's house. It went well and the precious documents were safe under lock and key in a massive vault three stories below ground somewhere in London.

Martha was elbow-deep in making pies. She'd been busy fiddling with her recipe since ten o'clock that morning. A loud knock signaled someone was at their front door.

"Will you get it?" Martha yelled from the kitchen.

Helen called back, "I'm on my way!"

Helen peeked through the half-moon window at the top of the door and saw Lana Chason standing on the flagstone doorstep, shivering. Throwing the door open, smiling broadly, Helen said, "Get in here, girl. It's freezing out there."

"Oh, it is nice to see you again, Helen." Lana's beautiful Louisiana accent warmed up the snug room, even more than it already was.

"Would you like something hot to drink? Martha's been baking all morning and we have oodles of things to eat. I bought some great coffee in Manhattan last week," Helen said, plying refreshment like any good Southerner would do when a guest arrives.

"I would love something to take the chill off. My blood's too thin for this cold Yorkshire winter." Lana stood by the stoked fire and rubbed her well-manicured hands for warmth.

"Do I hear the dulcet tones of a lady from New Orleans?" Martha asked, coming down the hall. Upon seeing Lana standing in her living room, Martha threw her hands up and said with a welcoming smile, "I thought that was you, Lana. What are you up to fraternizing with the competitors?"

Lana laughed good-humoredly and gave Martha a hug.

"I don't know what it is about this place, but every time I come to town, someone dies." She shivered.

Martha and Helen nodded mutely in agreement. All three women, for an instant, stood dumbly in the room, but Helen broke the somber silence. Putting a new log on the fire, she said, "It was an odd death, Lana. Saundra Johns looked the picture of health."

"She was," Lana said in a matter-of-fact way.

Both Helen and Martha immediately focused their eyes on her.

"Why do you say so?" Martha asked.

"Because not more than twenty minutes before she…died," Lana shot them an uncomfortable look, "she was talking with a man from the press. Saundra obviously knew him well. I overheard her telling him to meet her later at her hotel. It didn't sound like they were planning a menu."

"Hmm," Martha said with a grin, "Saundra got around."

"If I were a betting woman, I'd say so," Lana agreed. "But that wasn't all. They were talking flirtatiously and the man said the spinning she was doing every day was paying off."

"So, she must have been in great shape to do spinning every day. That pretty much confirms our suspicion," Martha said.

"What suspicion?" Lana asked.

"That she was murdered."

Lana's mouth dropped open. "Murdered?"

"Oh, yeah. Someone must have popped something either into her drink or her food," Helen said.

"Come on girls," Martha turned and walked to the kitchen, "it's time for something to eat. We can talk in here."

They all trooped down the hall and made themselves comfortable around the table. The topic switched for a while to the recent nuptials of Lana and her wealthy diamond-merchant husband from Manhattan. Martha cut up one of her cherry pies and warmed the slices in her stove. Lana begged for a cup of coffee, so Helen boiled the water for the French press. There were great uproars of laughter while Lana told the story of how she wooed, or more like lassoed, her new husband.

Once everyone was settled with everything they needed, they jumped back into their earlier conversation. However, before they dug too deeply into the facts, another knock on the front door sounded, and Amos, Martha's tiny Maltipoo, went berserk barking.

"My, we are popular today, Helen," Martha said, standing up and heading back to the living area. Another loud knock sent Amos into a twirling dance and more barking.

"Hush!" Martha hissed. "Go to your bed and lie down." Amos didn't listen but sat back on her haunches and beat her fuzzy tail on the floor. Martha peeked out the window and saw Polly standing there.

"Get in here!" Martha cried upon opening the door and letting Polly hurry inside. "What on Earth are you doing here, Polly?"

Johns' mother was bundled from head to foot in everything warm she must have owned. She pulled off one of her hats and unwrapped a muffler from around her neck and mouth. As soon as she was free to talk, she grabbed both of Martha's forearms forcefully and locked a severely serious gaze on her face.

"I've got to talk with you, Martha. We were the ones closest to Saundra when she…died. I've been over to the constabulary and Merriam told me Saundra was poisoned."

Martha nodded with a grim expression. "I thought so. I'm so, so sorry, Polly. This must be horrible for you and Merriam."

Polly, never taking her grip off Martha's arms, shook her.

"You don't get it, Martha. We were the two people closest to her. This isn't good. We've got to remember everything that happened."

"Okay, okay, Polly," Martha said soothingly. "We can do that. Come on let's sit down and we can go over it again."

Polly Johns looked terrified. She let go of Martha's arms and sat down in one of the oversized, upholstered chairs. Putting both of her hands together in a gesture of prayer, she turned her gaze back up to Martha.

"There are only three people who would have wanted her dead: Merriam, me and...you, Martha."

CHAPTER 148

Patrick Knells waited for the electric kettle to finish heating. He was thirty-five years old, divorced for five years and fairly good-looking, with sandy brown hair, five-foot-eleven in height and a lean build from jogging every day. He'd been dateless for over six months, and his mother had given up on ever knowing the joy of grandchildren. Patrick Knells wanted something more, but he didn't know how to find it.

He'd been focusing his attention out the second-story window of the Marsden-Lacey Constabulary watching two tall men meander down one of the medieval alleyways, pulling a fir tree as long as both of them put together. It was Christmas, after all, so they must be taking it somewhere for some purpose he thought to himself. His mind flitted back to those Christmases of his childhood. Something in this village awakened his nostalgic side.

The pot switched off on its own, awakening him again to the present. He poured some of the steaming water into a mug and decided to wait until the tea was finished steeping before he went back down to meet Chief Johns.

"Hello," came a friendly, young male voice from behind him. Knells swung around to see a pleasant-faced youth of about nineteen smiling brightly at him. Being on the force for over fifteen years, he'd lost a lot of his enthusiasm for the job, but the kid standing in front of him made him think of himself at that age, full of energy and drive to succeed.

"Hello. I'm Inspector Knells," he said holding out his hand to the junior officer.

"Sam Berry, sir. I saw you arrive. If you need anything, anything at all, I'm at your service."

"Well, Berry, thank you. How long have you been working here at Marsden-Lacey?"

"Almost a half year, sir. I've finished my first semester of police training. I...I would like to do an internship in Leeds someday. That's where the real action happens," Sam said, obviously, in awe of the officer from a metropolitan area like Leeds.

Knells wagged his head back and forth. "The action is right here, Berry. Were you at the Village Hall when the victim was killed yesterday?"

"Yes sir, I'm on the cooking team."

"Cooking team?" Knells asked, his eyebrows knitting together.

"Yeah, the Pudding and Pie Bake-Off team for the constabulary: Constable Waters, Chief Johns and Constable Endicott and I."

The new inspector from Leeds picked up his tea mug and took a sip. He thought for a second or two of how nice it would be to work in a place where people actually liked their police officers enough to see them as everyday citizens. An idea occurred to him.

"Berry, I've got to meet with your Chief. Where's a good place to have a bite to eat afterwards?"

"Easy, my aunt's teashop or The Traveller's Inn. Great food, either way. I'd be happy to take you there after work."

"If you're still here when I get back, I'd appreciate it. I'll be going to visit with a few local people for further questioning the rest of the day. Should be back around six this evening."

"I'll be here. Constable Waters has me on lock down until seven tonight. She's a veritable chain gang warden when it comes to serving my time."

Walking past Sam, Knells laughed and said, "Better get used to it, Berry. Every superior you have from here on out will make it their mission in life to hold your backside to the work fire."

Sam fell in step with Knells and walked with him to the Chief's office. At his door, Sam said he'd watch for him later, and the teenager disappeared down the hall. Knells knocked on the Chief's door.

"Come in," a gruff voice called from inside.

Knells opened the door and introduced himself.

"Yeah, your supervisor, Superintendent Lyons, just rang off. You'd better let me see your badge, Inspector Knells. I've had a bit of trouble in the past with being too trusting."

The men getting the formalities out of the way, discussed the situation of the murder, the evidence, and the process Inspector Knells used to manage his investigation.

"I've been looking into your divorce and I've spoken with your solicitor. He says your wife was asking for a substantial amount. You were going to have to sell your home. It's been in your family a couple of centuries."

Knells watched Johns' face for signs of discomfort. He wasn't disappointed.

"You're going to find out Saundra and I were not on the best of terms. I was extremely upset about selling my home, but I'd come to terms with it after talking with my mother. She lives there as well. I'd already spoken with a realtor, Mr. Crabtree, about listing the farm. It was a done-deal in my mind."

"Why were you divorcing your wife?"

"We hadn't lived together in over five years. Saundra left to live in London because she didn't like rural life and I...I was a bit of a disappointment to her."

"How so?"

"When we married, she expected my career to take me to a city like London. Saundra was a successful chef, as you know, and she wanted a more cosmopolitan lifestyle. I realized about two years into the marriage, I wanted to stay here. It was only a matter of time, after that."

Knells pondered on the similarity between his and Johns' situation, but it was reversed in regard to the players. He, too, had married, but his wife wanted the quieter life of a rural home. They'd separated after ten years of sullen hostility. He wished he'd understood then what he understood now.

"Please tell me how your mother took the news about moving from the farm?" he asked.

"I thought, quite honestly, she would have been extremely upset, but she was fine. She told me she wanted me to be free from Saundra. I know you're going to jump on that last comment, but Mum was peaceful about giving up the farm. She said people are more important than things."

The inspector from Leeds didn't speak. He considered the last statement, feeling the weight of it. Sacrifice had received bad press for the last one hundred years. It hadn't been politically correct since the 1960s. Love was sacrifice, but no one was comfortable with that notion of love anymore.

"Thank you, Chief. I'd like to speak with your mother and with…," he looked down at a hand-sized notebook with names he'd written into it, "a Mrs. Martha Littleword."

Knells lifted his gaze at the right moment he knew would be the most significant. The muscles in Johns' jaw tightened with the mention of the woman's name.

"Anything you want to tell me about our Mrs. Littleword?"

"Simple. I love her."

"Well," Knells said, taken aback by the candid statement, "congratulations. She feels the same way?"

"I think so; well, I thought so. I'd been reluctant to discuss my situation with Saundra…"

"Why's that?"

Johns sat back in his chair. His color rose up through his neck and into his cheeks. Knells waited. His own heart beat sped up. He'd found the sweet spot in the interrogation.

Taking a deep breath, Johns began, "I loved my wife. When she left, she was pregnant. I was ecstatic at the thought of having a family. Saundra was scared. We'd waited, in my opinion, too long to start a family, but I wanted Saundra not to feel pressured. She never told me what happened, but two months later, she called from London. She'd lost the baby."

Knells had enough truths to begin to build a case against Johns, but no proof. He gently encouraged Johns to continue.

"Did you want her back?"

"Yes, I did. I went to see her. She was living in London and when I got to the flat she shared with another person, I realized she was living with a man, not a woman. It was over. Neither she nor I talked about divorce, though, for another three years. I asked first."

"Why?'

"Saundra told me she wasn't coming back to Marsden-Lacey. She'd left the other man and had moved on to her second lover. My own personal life wasn't much in the way of successful. Living in a village, everyone knows your business. Everyone assumed I was divorced. I wanted to be solid on that point with people."

Johns glanced up at his interrogator. Knells nodded his understanding at what the man meant.

"I've got an ex-wife, too, Chief. It's hard to put yourself back out there."

"Yes, but in the last few months or so, there's been one person I've begun to fancy. It wasn't until Mrs. Littleword, Martha, came into my life, that I knew I'd met someone special." As Johns finished his sentence, his face lit up with a brief flare of humor.

"Did you murder your wife?" Knells said. His words acting like an astringent on the previous emotionally charged conversation.

Johns' lost his momentary ember-like glow of happiness.

"No," he said flatly. "I had everything ahead of me as of . yesterday before Saundra died. I was going to be free. Free to be with the woman I wanted."

"You have to admit, the best murderers are cops. They know what we're going to look for and how to avoid stupid mistakes.

Your wife's death was in the middle of a crowd, lots of people jostling each other, in other words, damn difficult to investigate."

"I'm a cop," Johns agreed. "I also know how justice catches up with people. Carrying that around until I was caught would have been another heavy load to carry. I've been doing that too long as it is."

"Precisely, Chief. Double edge sword wasn't it? One that cuts both ways."

Knells stood up and reached across the desk offering his hand to Johns to shake. Johns stood as well and accepted the investigator's offer of peace.

"I'm at your disposal, Knells. Let me know what you need. I've requested the video footage from the television crews who were here yesterday. Should be sometime this afternoon when we get them."

"Thank you, Chief. I'll look forward to seeing them soon."

The new investigator picked up his mug and left Johns' office. He didn't hurry. He planned on being around Marsden-Lacey for a long, long time.

CHAPTER 19

The elderly man was exhausted. The lack of movement and days of being held inside the claustrophobic room was beginning to take its toll on his health. He recognized the part of the house where they were holding him. It was the servants' quarters from when there was a huge retinue of hired help to keep the massive estate running. These rooms hadn't seen humans on a regular basis for over eighty years.

Lord Henry Tolbert Farthingay, the owner of Greenwoods Abbey, was well into his eighties and he'd lost his wife, Abigail, over thirty years ago. His interest in the great house and its land had never been much. For most of his life, he and Abigail lived abroad in places like Sydney, Australia, and South Africa. They preferred the modern and the heat over Greenwood's ancient Englishness. When Abigail died, he had become nostalgic for the place of his youth, so he had returned to his ancestral home.

As he lay on his bed, hearing the horrible girl's music coming out of the tiny plugs she kept stuffed in her ears, he wished to be free from this place forever. The crackling sound of the music was repetitive, primitive and without any effort to impart beauty. He rolled his head over to see the wall. At least, the wall was a canvas for his imagination or his memory. Since Abigail's death, they often intertwined.

"It's time for you medicine," Melissa said, hovering over him like a vulture. He knew she wanted to be free of him just as he wanted to be free of her.

"I promise to be perfectly quiet and not to move, if you'll let me sit in the chair and read--no medicine, only reading," he asked.

Melissa stepped back and sunk down on another bed, with one leg underneath her and her back against the wall. He knew she was studying him for signs indicating his true intentions, so he let his body relax and breathed evenly.

"Okay, but I won't remove your shackles."

"That's fine. I don't need them to be removed," he agreed.

Soon, he was sitting comfortably in an upright position. His head felt light and dizzy. Four days had passed since he'd been allowed up. Melissa, per Brickstone's orders, had stuffed him with drugs and he'd lost all sense of time and place. The dizziness was becoming worse.

A constriction in his chest and a tingling numbness in his right arm signaled the onset of what he recognized as a heart attack. With swift awareness, Lord Henry knew he was dying. He didn't say a word, but shut his eyes to better bear the pain. He wanted to go.

"Come with me," a woman's voice said above him.

He looked up, to see a pretty face with auburn ringlets bending down over him. The lovely lady smiled at him and at her throat he saw a magnificent diamond and ruby brooch pinned to her collar. Was she the woman in the library's portrait?

"Where am I going?" he said, standing up and feeling no pain whatsoever. Staring down at his hands, he didn't recognize them. They were young and free of the lumpy veins and brown spots he'd come to see each day.

The woman took his hand and warmth spread through his entire being. She tilted her head thoughtfully, with a loving smile and said, "Why, you're going home, of course. Abigail is there. She's waiting for you."

He followed her past Melissa and out through his familiar wall into the sunlit snowy landscape beyond. In an instant, the full, wondrous majesty of the natural world gripped him and he knew its miracle. He felt humbled and shamed for ever taking such beauty for granted.

As they walked, the beautiful woman talked to him. He never saw her mouth move, but he understood her completely. She told him he would be happy and soon see others he'd known and loved. They came to a place far from the house, where a ruin sat beside a frozen lake and she stopped.

"I have to go."

"Where are you going?" he asked.

"It's my job to watch over my family. You are one of mine. I love you, go in peace."

He watched her go and soon she disappeared. Her whiteness first blended with, and was eventually erased by, the white fields of snow. A tap on his shoulder caused him to turn around. There stood Abigail, young and radiant.

"Come on," she said taking his hand. "Let's go home."

The care of Henry Farthingay had passed from one protective, loving soul and to another.

CHAPTER 20

Señor Agosto, along with Alistair Turner and Perigrine Clark, was working to create a festive feeling in the Pudding and Pie Bake-Off's new venue, the Marsden-Lacey High School gymnasium.

"The smell of used socks, angst and athletic shoes," Alistair was saying to Perigrine, "reminds me of my days at Colchester as a lad."

"It's intolerable!" Agosto fumed loudly from his perch on a stool. "How can this offensive odor of human perspiration allow the nose to do its job in choosing the best dishes?"

The diminutive chef from Spain waved his hands high above his head in a fit of temper. He'd been setting up the separate working areas for the teams, but his mood had become increasingly black with the abrupt changes of yesterday and the loss of a quality judge.

"We have the Christmas tree set in its stand. The smell of pine may have a cleansing effect," Perigrine mused.

Agosto studied the tall tree and let out a dramatic sigh. He hopped down from the step stool he'd been using to work at one of the prep areas, and walked with quick, short steps over to the tree's place in the corner of the huge room.

"We do not have time to decorate such a behemoth!" he cried.

"You don't have to," a woman said, her tone indicating a certain comfortableness with command.

Agosto, Alistair, and Perigrine turned to find Miss Purcell, the indomitable Headmistress of Marsden-Lacey's High School standing at one of the main entrance doors to the gym.

"And who are you, madam?" Agosto asked with one eyebrow arched. Though only slightly over five and a half feet tall, he gave the illusion of great height.

"Miss Purcell is my name. We have not met, Señor. I am the Headmistress here." She bowed her head regally at Agosto. With a warm smile for Perigrine and Alistair, she said, "It's always good to see you, Clark and Turner. We've enjoyed the refreshing water feature near the faculty's outside dining area. You did a beautiful job. Thank you."

Alistair and Perigrine crossed the distance to where she'd stopped. Agosto busied himself with counting out chairs for the judges, press and dignitaries who would occupy them during the Bake-Off.

"The students will decorate the tree today, if you like," Miss Purcell said to Perigrine and Alistair. She was wearing a perfectly pressed blue business suit, with random cat hairs clinging to the fabric.

"Thank you. Any help will be greatly appreciated. We're under the gun so to speak," Alistair said.

"So, Purcell, you've signed up to make at least two-thirds of Marsden-Lacey's population your potential enemy," Perigrine said cheerfully as he adjusted his bow tie.

"I did that the minute I became a Headmistress, Clark. On any given day, I've got, at the very least, a couple of families upset with me. Judging comes naturally, and I've been chief cook at every school fundraiser for the last ten years." Giving an appraising look at Señor Agosto, she added, "I'm comfortable with fussy, disagreeable types."

Perigrine and Alistair stayed mute deigning not to raise the temperamental Spaniard's ire, but their eyes widened at the comment. Purcell smiled wickedly.

Agosto's hearing was excellent and was tuned to the conversation taking place across the room. At the Headmistress' comment, he puffed up considerably, taking it as a slight. He puckered his mouth, marched to where the other three stood, and raising a steely gaze to the eyes of the female paragon of educational fortitude, he said, "I am not deaf, madam. I heard your insinuation so callous and undeserved regarding me." He raised his eyebrows with a look of hauteur. "Your gymnasium smells of young men's feet."

"It's a gym. It has lots of young men *and* young women's feet in it every day," she said, her own irritation with the irascible chef beginning to shine through on her usually impassive face.

"If we air out the room before the event tomorrow, it should be fine," Alistair offered.

"No!" Agosto stamped his foot. He paced a circular area with his head down while the other three watched bemused by his animated manner.

They had turned to chatting about Paris and the upcoming trip for the students, when out of nowhere Agosto said triumphantly, "I have it! We must wash the floor with a cleansing agent of water, lemon, and crushed thyme. It will work!"

He smiled brilliantly, as if he'd solved the greatest conundrum since the invention of the electric mixer. His temper passed, he turned his attention to Miss Purcell.

"Will you allow this, madam? We must have a fresh room for the noses," he touched the side of his own prodigious sniffer, while proffering the Headmistress an amicable smile.

"I don't see why not," she said graciously. "I'll send two of my better young men to help you. They'll be here during the study hour."

Miss Purcell bowed her head and said her farewells to the three gentlemen. The Bake-Off was going to chug along, despite the setbacks. Agosto busied himself with the preparation of his floor-cleaning fluid, while Perigrine and Alistair continued the setting up. Maybe the choir students would make it to Paris, after all. Only 'thyme' would tell.

Scene Break

After Helen, Lana and Martha restored Polly's emotional equilibrium by plying her with hot chamomile tea and four oatmeal cookies, they sat discussing what each of them had seen the day of the meet and greet.

"Polly, did you notice anyone unusual or see anything?" Helen asked.

"I've lived in Marsden-Lacey my entire life, dear. I recognized almost everyone except for the outsiders. There were a lot of people from the Press."

Amos growled and barked at the front door.

"Oh, don't tell me," Martha said laughing, "that we've got another lost soul wandering around outside in this storm."

She got up to look out the window. Mrs. Cuttlebirt's tiny dog, Pepper, was barking and pawing at his front door. Looking at the clock on her wall to see the time, Martha quickly looked back outside again.

"Something wrong?" Lana asked.

"It's eleven-thirty and I usually see Mrs. Cuttlebirt walking her dog, Pepper. I don't see her outside, but Pepper is, which is strange because it's so cold. I'd better go check on Mrs. Cuttlebirt. She might be sick. That's what neighbors are for."

"You want me to come with you?" Helen offered.

"Nah, stay here and work out who killed Saundra. Try and pin it on someone other than Polly and me."

Everyone was making appropriate sarcastic comments to Martha's request, as she let herself out of her front door.

The soft snow was still falling and its heavy blanket lay thick and pillowy across her walled garden. It was difficult to not stoop down and scoop up a bit of it to taste. Snow was a rarity in central Arkansas when she was growing up, so she always had a firm appreciation of the wonder it.

As Martha opened Mrs. Cuttlebirt's ancient iron gate, Pepper came running up to her. She scooped the tiny Yorkshire terrier up. Even with his red sweater on, Pepper was still shaking from the cold. Martha stuck him inside her coat and took two steps toward Mrs. Cuttlebirt's front door. As she used the knocker, the door swung open. Martha's heart beat faster. Something was wrong.

"Mrs. Cuttlebirt? Hello! Mrs. Cuttlebirt, are you here?" she called.

Nothing. A pungent odor wafted up, causing Martha to turn her head to the outside air and take a deep breath. Her instincts told her to stay outside.

Pushing the door open to see the entire room, she saw a woman's arm extending from behind a settee. It must be Mrs. Cuttlebirt's. Pepper squirmed in Martha's arms, trying to get down. She held him firmly. With the door open, cold air filled the room rapidly. A sudden gust of wind blew the door back against the wall with a bang, causing Martha to jump and scream.

She heard Amos' muted barking, even though he was inside her house. A sensation of fear made Martha walk outside. There was death clinging to the air of Mrs. Cuttlebirt's cottage.

"Hey! I heard you scream," Helen was calling from Flower Pot's front door. "Are you okay?"

"No! Call the police and the ambulance. I think Mrs. Cuttlebirt needs emergency help. Don't let Amos out. I think something is wrong about the house. It may be a gas leak."

Martha walked back to her own garden's gate, and soon she heard the siren of an ambulance, and other sirens following. Once they arrived, the team of two jumped out and Martha went over and stopped them from going inside.

"I think there's gas in the house. I shouldn't think it would be a good idea to go in. It may not be safe," she said over the other sirens from police and fire vehicles arriving.

The two paramedics waited until the fire chief stomped through the snow to where they stood. Martha was beginning to shiver, but she waited. Soon, Chief Johns and Sergeant Endicott, along with a new man Martha didn't recognize, were walking toward them. Johns shot her a look. She couldn't be sure of the meaning behind it.

Soon he extricated himself from the others and came over to her. The new man watched him with curiosity, Martha thought.

"Did you find the body, Martha?" Johns asked, a hint of worry in his tone.

"Yes, I did. There's something else in your tone, Merriam. What's going on, and who's the fresh face you brought with you?" she countered.

His voice dropped to a whisper, "It's the inspector from the Leeds Constabulary who's taken over the murder investigation."

"Your mother told us. Helen and I thought she'd been killed, too. Who in the world would have wanted to murder your wife?"

Martha and Johns' eyes met. Unspoken words hovered between them.

"Well, after meeting her, I can see she may have had a few enemies," Martha admitted.

"They'll check for gas. Did you smell anything when you went inside?" Johns asked. They both watched as two firemen started to go inside.

"It smelled like bitter almonds, if I could call it that," Martha said simply.

Johns turned on her with a serious look. He grabbed her by the shoulders.

"Did you breathe any of it?" He turned away still holding her and yelled for one of the paramedics to come quickly.

"What's wrong, Merriam? Why are you acting so excited?" Martha demanded.

"Hush for a minute," he said softly and yelled over to where the fire chief was talking with one of his people.

"James! It's cyanide gas! Get your men out of there!"

Every one of the emergency people, the police and the firemen milling about the outside of Mrs. Cuttlebirt's house stopped cold in their tracks. Then like there'd been a snap in the universal time continuum, they all moved quickly and the fire chief was shouting orders at the top of his lungs.

"Go inside, Martha," Johns commanded. "I'm sending one of the paramedics in to give you oxygen. This is serious. This is murder."

CHAPTER 21

The day was beginning to ebb away as the forensic team and the police brought in powerful work lights and set them up outside of Flower Pot Cottage. Martha was told to shower head to toe and put her clothes into a special plastic bag to avoid any contamination within her house. Johns was handling this investigation and Knells decided it was a perfect time to re-interview Martha and Polly about Saundra's murder.

He'd asked politely if Martha was up to talking after the paramedic finished her oxygen treatment. Helen and Lana stayed in the kitchen, while Polly sat wrapped in Martha's favorite fuzzy blanket holding Pepper, Mrs. Cuttlebirt's orphaned terrier in the oversized chair by the fire.

"Feeling better?" he asked Martha. For a second, he found himself watching how her hair caught the light of the fire. He righted himself as he saw her nod in the affirmative.

"Do you remember, since your statement yesterday, anything new about the period of time you spent talking with Saundra Johns?" he asked, watching her face for hesitations or evasive gestures.

"We've been discussing it," she indicated Polly, petting Pepper, who was sleeping soundly. "Helen and Lana, too, but the only thing I feel that might be possible is she was poisoned."

Knells sat back a bit in his chair. "Why so?"

"She grabbed at her throat and said she couldn't breathe followed by the convulsions. That's not a stroke, in my opinion," Martha said, looking Knells directly in the eyes.

"Perceptive, Mrs. Littleword. She died of poisoning, cyanide poisoning in fact."

Martha's face went white. She sat back into the softness of her couch. "Like Mrs. Cuttlebirt," she whispered.

The cell phone rang beside her. Glancing down, she saw that it was Kate calling.

"Can I take this? It's my daughter."

"Of course," he said. He had a hard time taking his eyes from Martha. She was extremely feminine and, he couldn't help noticing, well formed.

Martha tapped the phone's face and said, "Kate? Hi, baby. What's going on?"

Polly and Knells busied themselves with whatever was available, picking lint from the blanket for Polly and scratching the cat, Vera's, furry head for Knells.

"No, Kate. That's fine, sweetheart. I'll make sure to be there on Wednesday. I can't wait to see you, too. Santa's probably got something already here for you," Martha said teasingly.

Knells and Polly exchanged bemused glances. Polly huddled back down into her warm cocoon with her new best canine friend.

"Bye, baby. I love you. Stay warm, and if the friend you're bringing home is of the male version, tell him your mother says he'd better be doing a good job of keeping you safe, or I'll hurt him."

Polly chuckled and Knells flashed a smile at Martha's last warning. The call over, Martha put the phone down and sighed.

"I'm worried. Kate's going to be home in less than six days. If there's a murderer running around, I need you people," she looked severely at Knells, "to get on the stick and find out who did it. It's more dangerous in Marsden-Lacey than Mexico City these days," Martha fumed.

Knells saw the sincerity on her face and heard it in her voice. He was a good judge of character after the years of being a cop, and he knew when someone was putting on.

Martha got up, and in so doing, tripped over his foot causing her to lose her balance. She fell and Knells quickly reached to grab her. The front door opened as Martha fell into Knells' arms. For a brief moment, he could smell her fresh, clean hair and the soft, warmth of her skin. Chief Johns stood rooted to the spot.

Knells released his grip and lifted her easily back into an upright position.

"Sorry, Mrs. Littleword for my feet getting in the way," he said apologetically.

Martha, standing in the middle of the room on her own two feet, nodded to him and said, "Thanks. No worries." Turning to Merriam, she asked, "Is everything done? Did they take Mrs. Cuttlebirt away?"

Johns shot a hard look at Knells, then relaxed his tense frame and said in a gentle tone, "Yes, I'm sorry, Martha. I know how you cared for her. They'll take the body to Leeds for forensics to analyze." The last statement, he said more to Knells than to Martha.

Knells stood up. "I need to finish these interviews and get back to the station. One of your junior officers has promised to show me a good place to eat for supper."

"Well, have a seat, young man, and let's get this over with," Polly said commandingly.

Somewhat taken aback by her forcefulness, Knells obediently settled himself again in a chair. He took out his notepad and turned to Polly. She didn't let him ask a question, but instead started with, "I first met Saundra on a cold day. If I'd had my wits about me, I would have known it was to be the beginning of a bitter time for us all. You see…"

Johns and Martha slipped away down to the tiny office at the back of the cottage. Once the door was shut, Johns asked tersely, "What was *he*," pointing back in the direction of the living room, "doing with you on his lap?"

Martha countered, "Why didn't you tell me *you* had a wife?"

"What's that got to do with you sitting on his lap?"

"She told me yesterday before she…died, that you'd been begging her to take you back?" Martha said, giving him a mindful flick of her hand to his chest.

He grabbed her hand, holding it, causing her to become still in his grasp. Johns let his head drop in a gesture of frustration and confusion. He pulled her to him.

"Martha, please don't think for one moment that anything, anything that woman may have said to you was true. I'd come to despise her and pity her. There was no love between us, and I intended to give her everything I owned just to be free of her."

The two of them were quiet for a moment. Martha said softly, "Why didn't you tell me about being married? It's a simple question, Merriam. You owe me an answer."

"From the minute I met you, I knew the kind of woman you were. Last fall, during the Faberge-gypsy craziness, I realized my feelings for you."

"I understand," Martha said, nodding with playful cheekiness, "there's been others caught in my web of magnetic charm."

Johns smiled down into her upturned, vivacious face. He finished, "Yes, that's it exactly, Littleword. I couldn't resist you, and I couldn't get my wife to give me a divorce. I didn't want you to drop me like a hot potato and you would have if you'd known about my being married. It's not an excuse for not telling you. I know that."

Martha nodded.

He continued. "So, I've been trying to move heaven and hell to get Saundra to agree to a settlement. She finally gave it to me."

"She was going to give you the divorce?" Martha asked hopefully.

"Yes, for a price."

"What did she want?"

"The farm," he answered.

Martha sat down in her desk chair. She didn't take her eyes off of Johns' face. He didn't say anything.

"The farm means so much to you and Polly."

"No," he said, his eyes intense with emotion, "it doesn't mean anything compared to losing you."

"That's why they've taken you off the case, isn't it? You're their number one suspect," she said pointedly.

"You're wondering if they have it right?" he asked.

"No. If you wanted to be free, the last thing you would have wanted was to have someone's death on your hands," Martha said simply.

Johns took the two steps to where Martha sat in her chair. He pulled her up into his arms and kissed her with a passion he'd never known for any woman before. She was his true other half. She knew him and he wanted only her. Their embrace was halted by a sharp rap on the office door.

"Lana's leaving. She has to get back to the hotel. Her husband's supposed to be back from London. Hey! Can you hear me? Are you in there?"

Martha and Johns, still holding each other, laughed softly.

"Okay! Helen," Martha called. "I'll be right out. Merriam and I are talking."

Martha looked up at Johns with a soft expression and said, "You'd better be going."

"I don't want to," he replied.

"Go find who killed your wife and, I promise, you can stay," she said warmly.

He bent down to kiss her again, and she put a finger over his lips.

"I'm of the belief, Merriam, that when we do things the right way, good things follow. I want the best for you and for me. We've got to do this right. Do you understand?"

He nodded. She slipped free from his arms. Opening the office door, they went outside to say goodbye to Lana. Polly and Knells were finishing up.

"Do you still have time to finish with a few questions, Mrs. Littleword?" Knells asked.

"Sure," she sat down. The questions were much like the ones she'd already answered. Knells wanted to know about her work, what she and Helen were doing in Warwickshire, and reminded her to tell him if she remembered anything in the future. He handed her his card.

When he left, Johns, Polly, and Pepper went with him, leaving Helen and Martha alone.

"Polly has really taken to Pepper," Helen said crawling back into her chair by the fire.

"I know. She'll be buying sweaters for him soon." Martha threw another log on her fire and sat on the sofa. "The quiet feels good, but would you like to get some fresh air?" Martha asked.

"What's your idea?"

"I'd like to go to St. Elizabeth's. Feel like a walk? It's not too far."

Helen stood up from her seat. "Let's go. I need to stretch my legs."

They layered themselves with lots of warm outerwear and pulled on fur-lined boots. The night was calm and full of stars.

For a long while, they walked in silence until Helen heard some sniffling coming from Martha.

"Hey, are you okay?" she asked.

"I'm going to miss her, Mrs. Cuttlebirt, I mean."

There wasn't much one could say or do, but Helen did what any good friend would; she put her arms around the crying Martha, gave her a firm hug and told her she understood. In between life and death, if one is lucky, there is love and friendship.

CHAPTER 22

As he sat in his warm car enjoying the heated seats, Ricky Brickstone's cell phone rang again. It was Melissa. She'd called six times in the last hour. He was tired of her drama, her neediness and most of all, her. Six calls usually signified something of import, so with a martyred sigh, he tapped the 'accept' button on his phone's face.

"Yes," he slurred.

"He's dead," came the whispered female voice on the other end.

"Thank you for letting me know. I loved Mr. Tickles and I appreciate your wonderful care," Ricky replied.

He hoped the simpleton on the other end would hear the tone of his voice and not go any further in her conversation. Ricky waited for her reply.

"You're welcome. We hope you'll come soon to collect his body or we can have it sent to a pet crematorium. It's, of course, your decision," Melissa said, her intonation more like a first-year drama student than a believable veterinarian's assistant.

Internally, Ricky relaxed. Melissa was thick, but to her credit, this time, she'd gotten the gist. Better not to leave the authorities with any evidence to levy against him later. The digital world was full of potential potholes and phones were the best way for someone to slip up and fall into one.

"I'll wait to see you. When can we expect you?" Melissa asked.

Ricky thought for a moment before answering. A brilliant idea leapt into his mind. He remembered the old lime kiln on Greenwoods' back acreage.

"Soon. Thank you again."

He hit 'end', leaving Melissa probably staring at her phone in utter disbelief. A chuckle rumbled in his throat at what her expression must have been. Ricky didn't care. It bought him time. Lord Percy was dead and Melissa wasn't needed anymore. He could have her help him drag the old man's body into the kiln and then…no more Melissa. The thought of it made Ricky smile. He was so relieved. Three problems solved. It had been an extremely productive day.

His black sedan slid onto the M1 motorway. He was Greenwoods bound and with good traffic, he'd be there in a couple of hours.

Scene Break

Polly and Johns straggled up to the front door of their family home. It had been an exhausting day. Johns knew his mother tried to do everything in her power not to let anyone pull double duty because of her age, but she was extremely tired and he wanted her to rest. The Bake-Off competition was starting early tomorrow at nine o'clock.

The house was cool inside. No fire had been built that morning and it felt like it. Johns checked the thermostat and upped the temperature to bring some needed warmth to the rooms.

"I'm ready for bed, Merriam," Polly said. She put her foot on the first riser of the stairs.

"Mum," her son spoke behind her, making her turn to look him in the face.

"Yes?"

"There going to look at us first in this investigation. You do understand? It may get ugly and people will talk behind our backs. Are you going to be okay?"

Johns' eyes lifted up, his expression unsure, with worry pulling at the laugh lines at the corners. His gaze locked with hers.

"I don't care what other people say. People always need something to talk about. I didn't kill her, Merriam," she said tiredly. "I don't step on spiders either. Even when I know they'll try and crawl into bed with me, bite me if given the chance, and leave their eggs to threaten me in the future with their venomous offspring. I still don't kill them."

Her expression was quiet, serene in its dispassion. "I put them under a glass and lift them up with a piece of paper and toss them back out into the garden, letting them be preyed on as they prey on others. Nature has a way of taking care of itself."

Polly smiled at her son. It was the way a mother, without words, tells a child everything is fine. She turned and went into the darkness of the upper floor of the house. He heard her bedroom door click softly shut.

Satisfied she'd be okay, Johns went over to the inglenook fireplace and filled it with wood. He lit it, went to the pantry, and pulled out one of the Hefeweizen beers his mother brewed. Rinsing a glass with cool water, he poured the yeasty beer, making sure the glass was tilted. He swirled the bottle a bit, catching the rest of the yeast in a tiny tornado, and finished pouring the contents into the glass.

The fire was crackling and popping nicely. Johns sat down in his chair and propped his legs up on the hearth fender. He watched the logs catch flame and considered the murder of Saundra.

Since he knew it wasn't him, it had to be someone who would know how to access or use cyanide. God knows Saundra certainly had people who disliked her, but enough to kill her? What if she was in financial difficulties? She kept an expensive lifestyle. Possibly her money needs had put her in debt to the wrong people. Thugs would have shot her. This murder was done to shut her up quick, but why?

Johns lifted the glass to take a drink. He'd watched the videos sent over by the television crew. There'd been so many people in such a tight area, it would be impossible to see anyone put something in Saundra's drink. The few people who served at the refreshment table remembered Polly, Martha and Saundra talking. One man even recalled Martha handing Saundra her filled tea mug and overhearing snippets of the conversation, which was in line with what Martha and Polly had stated.

Tiny threads of different statements weaved a tapestry of possibilities in Johns' mind. Saundra was murdered deliberately; there was no doubt about it, and someone chose the Marsden-Lacey Pudding and Pie Bake-Off for its venue. Public places are much better to kill in, of course, if you want other people to be suspects. Johns thought about the tea mug. How many people had their hands on it? His mind snagged on a statement thread.

Getting up, he put the beer glass in the sink. He took out his phone and called Constable Waters. The mobile rang.

"Marsden-Lacey Constabulary. How may I help you?" came her voice on the other end.

"Waters, would you please send me the statements from the people working the refreshment table?" he asked in his usual perfunctory tone.

There was a cough from Waters and she hesitatingly replied, "Well, Chief, I've been told to not share any of the investigative items or papers with you."

"Why" he barked, "I'm the Chief. Who the hell told you that?"

"Detective Investigator Knells. He says you're on suspension until further notice." It was dead quiet for a second. Donna said conspiratorially, "You've been banned from the building."

Johns stared dumbly at the fire roaring in the massive stone fireplace.

"Chief?" Donna asked. "Are you there?"

"I'm here."

She whispered, "Would you be able to meet me tomorrow at my house? I've got the day off, as you know, and I think we should talk. I've got the competition until noon. Would one o'clock work?"

"I'll be there," he said firmly into the phone. "Waters?"

"Yes, sir?"

"Thank you."

"Absolutely. I'll see you tomorrow."

The phone went quiet in his hand and it occurred to him that something in Detective Inspector Knells' agenda didn't ring true. He dialed another number.

"Hi Chief Johns," came a female voice. "You know how I love to work the late shift, don't you. The morgue can be so invigorating this time of night."

CHAPTER 23

Friday morning came with cheerful sunshine and a glorious clear sky. The first round of the Pudding and Pie Bake-Off was well underway. Señor Agosto was like a happy, bouncing flea jumping from one team's workstation to the next. He made entertaining statements to the hovering cameras in whispered tones about the difficulty and complexities of creating the perfect pie crust. There had actually been a few ooh's and aha's from the spectator-packed bleachers.

Helen, Martha, Polly and Mr. O'Grady were almost completely done with their traditional meat pie. No one was allowed to put their dishes into the ovens until Agosto called time.

"He's fearsome," Martha said, nudging Polly.

"I heard from my best friend, Jane," Polly whispered, "he's threatened to throw the pies into the rubbish, if we so much as go over by a single second after he calls time."

Martha and Polly shifted their eyes over to study the energetic, bantam Spaniard. He was warning Harriet Berry, that their time was almost up. Harriet was flashing daggers at one of her team members, who hurriedly tried to whisk eggs for a wash for the crust.

"When he gets over here," Helen said softly, so that only the other three at the workstation could hear, "don't say anything. I've been watching, and anyone who tries to kiss-up to him has been given the evil eye. It could hurt our chances."

Martha opened her mouth to say something, potentially indignant, but both Polly and Helen simultaneously said firmly, "Don't do it."

Polly added, "I want to beat Harriet Berry. She's the best cook in Marsden-Lacey and everyone knows it. She was also the one in school who won our yearly cooking contests. Just once, I want to know I've got the chops to beat her. So, Martha, no talking to Agosto, got it?"

Martha gave her a sour look and said grumpily, "Got it."

Agosto plowed over to where they were standing. His aquiline nose held at a discerning level as he approached the table where their beautiful pie sat innocently upon a tidy workstation. Everyone knew, Agosto was fastidious about how a kitchen should be kept clean at all times. They were going for every possible angle in order to win the contest.

Agosto bent down and sniffed the pie, and taking out a hand-sized, leather-bound notepad, he made notations in it. The television cameras honed in upon the four bright-eyed competitors. Helen blushed and Polly stood straighter. But it was Mr. O'Grady who stole the show. He wore a pin on his white baker's jacket. It was a coronation pin for Queen Elizabeth II proudly worn over Mr. O'Grady's heart. When the cameras zoomed in on the dapper gentleman, he smiled broadly and pointed to the pin saying the words 'God Bless the Queen'.

The spectators caught O'Grady's charming declaration of affection for his monarch as they watched a camera close-up shot on the massive television screen at one end of the gym floor. The crowd cheered and clapped, and someone from the back of the room started singing the national anthem. Mr. O'Grady waved happily, and Polly rolled her eyes heavenward.

One of the interviewers, a woman, asked the team if they thought their chances were good to move on to the second round. Polly, Martha and Helen didn't speak at first. It was Polly who jumped in, saying, "We're just happy to be here," her statement reminiscent of an Oscar nominee's. Nobody dared move, but Martha squelched a snort of laughter in time, as Agosto's steely stare flashed onto her.

Finished with his inspection, he asked Alistair, Lana, and Mrs. Purcell to come over and do their evaluations. Everyone breathed a sigh of relief when Agosto quit their table.

Soon, every team's pie was baking in the oven. All that was left to do was to present their recipe plans for tomorrow and hope they'd be allowed to go on to the next round. The teams chatted and laughed with one another sharing their angst-riddled cooking stories from the last three hours.

"We should go ahead and take our recipes for the tea part of the competition to the judges' table," Martha said.

Helen's phone rang and she said, "Give me a minute. It's Mr. Brickstone, Lord Percy's nephew. I'll be right back."

She tapped the button. "Hello, Mr. Brickstone. How are you?"

"Doing well, Mrs. Ryes, thank you. I wanted to know how the transport of my manuscript went and when you'll be able to give me a complete valuation."

"Of course. Monday, my colleague and I are driving to London where Sinead Peters, the Hisox's agent, will meet us. I'm expecting one expert with an auction background and two other Shakespearean scholars who are extremely familiar with known works by Shakespeare. It'll take some time, with this type of find, more than a month."

"I see, Mrs. Ryes. You did say, though, you would be going down with your colleague to London?" he asked.

"Yes, I'll be sure to call you, as soon as the meeting is done," Helen added, not sure what he was asking.

"Fine, fine, I look forward to hearing from you. Enjoy your weekend. Are you still employed in the master chef competition?" he asked good-humouredly.

"It's not so masterly at the moment. Martha burnt one of our oven mitts and we had to stuff it into a drawer before the judge came by," Helen said, with a laugh.

"Well, I wish you all the best of luck, Mrs. Ryes and thank you again for your help in this matter."

Helen tapped the phone's end button and hurried back to the place where her team was standing. The pies were supposed to be coming out of the huge ovens in the cafeteria kitchen. Everyone was waiting to take their turn at collecting their dish. There was one last preparation to complete the pies. Soon everyone was finished and the pies were ready.

"Please take your pies to the judges' table and make sure your team card is with your entry. We don't want anyone disqualified for misrepresentation," Agosto said over the loud speaker.

All the teams reverently placed their pie with their team's card upon the table indicated. Everyone was to go and sit until the decisions were made. Three of the teams would go on to the next round, and three would be sent home. It was a room full of high expectations and nervous chatter.

Finally, Agosto climbed the stairs once more.

"We have made our collective decision," Agosto announced. "Please be ready to send your team's captain to collect your pie and afterwards each team, regardless of placement, will be photographed by Mr. Pogue, for the Marsden-Lacey Times."

A hushed excitement emanated from the crowd. People talked and bets were being made by some of the rowdier spectators. The television cameras panned the room showing the packed bleachers and the tense competitors huddled together in their individual teams.

"We'll call out your team's name," Agosto declared. "Our first team made a lovely traditional Yorkshire raised chicken and ham pie with an excellent hot water crust pastry. Berry's Bakers, please come up to the table."

The crowd went wild with cheers and applause. Harriet Berry's team, Berry's Bakers, clasped each other in a group hug. After the excitement abated, Harriet approached the table and accepted a handshake from Agosto, who beamed graciously from his elevated position on a compact platform. Harriet's team walked away for their picture to be taken.

Agosto cleared his throat, bringing the excited crowd back under his control. "Our next team tried a daring twist on an old favorite. They took a chance and added curry to a puffed pastry pie of mushrooms, cream, and chicken. Excellent presentation and a unique concept! It is...Tea Tarts!"

Amidst another uproar of applause from the bleachers, happy, jumping competitors congratulated one another, bringing the Bake-Off to a level of heightened anticipation. Who would win the last coveted spot? Helen, Martha, Polly and Mr. O'Grady each offered well wishes for The Tea Tarts as they trooped by to get their picture made for the paper.

"Here goes," Martha trilled with excitement. She crossed her fingers.

"Our last team delivered a true tour d'force. Their entry was a traditional English steak and Stilton pie. What gave it depth, in our opinion, was the fresh handling of the stout beer in the recipe. Please collect your pie The Dough Nuts!"

The spectators went over-the-top with their applause, bravos, and good shows. Polly kissed O'Grady right on the mouth causing him to turn bright red, while Helen and Martha wrapped each other in a delighted hug. With red cheeks and a light step, Polly went up to the waiting Agosto and accepted her pie. From the bleachers, came more well-wishes as Polly's team, The Dough Nuts, made their way to where the newspaper photographers waited to take their picture.

"Congratulations!" Piers said, coming up to The Dough Nuts. "Your culinary abilities must be spot on, for Agosto to wax on so long. I'd like a slice of that pie, Mrs. Ryes."

Helen forgot her usual distaste for public display and squeezing Piers' hand, stood on her toes and planted a kiss on his cheek.

"Forget the pie, I'll take more of that," he proffered his cheek for another kiss.

Polly leaned over to Helen and whispered in her ear, "You need to bring that bull home, Helen."

The corner of Helen's smile quivered and she whispered back, "Polly, I'm trying, now shhh."

What was left of the morning was spent talking with friends and visitors. All the competitors were in demand to discuss their dishes with curious recipe hounds. The Marsden-Lacey

Constabulary team was out which was sad because everyone knew they'd lost one of their best team members, Chief Johns.

"Donna, I'm sorry about this situation. You didn't get a fair shake with the competition," Martha said to Constable Waters.

"It's fine, Martha, we're kind of glad to be out. There's so much going on at work and at home. My youngest has been sick, and I want him better before Christmas. Also, with the Chief gone, things are out of sorts at the constabulary."

"Gone? What do you mean?" Martha asked, her tone confused.

Donna's voice dropped to a low voice, "Detective Inspector Knells has removed The Chief from the constabulary, pending the investigation into the death of his wife."

Martha couldn't help the shock showing on her face.

Donna continued, "He's off all investigations, even the one regarding Mrs. Cuttlebirt's murder. I'm going to see him, though, at one o'clock. I've asked him to come over to my house to talk about some things going on at the Constabulary."

"Under the table talk, right?" Martha asked.

"Yes, Knells may be trying to…displace Chief Johns. That's my feeling anyway. Mind you, it could be a mistaken impression on my part, but I think he would like to be the next Chief for Marsden-Lacey."

Martha leaned back and considered Donna thoughtfully. "Your instincts are dead-on, Donna. I had a faint inkling myself in that same direction. Both of us have picked up on it, so there's something to it."

"I've got to go," Donna said grudgingly. "It's almost twelve-thirty. The ride over to my house takes fifteen minutes and my house is probably a wreck. See you soon, Martha, and best of luck for tomorrow."

"Thank you, Donna."

The two women separated and were soon lost in the crowd. Martha made her way to where Helen and Polly were talking with Miss Purcell, the Headmistress-Judge.

"So, you're a brewer?" Miss Purcell was saying, "Using your own stout beer was an excellent decision. It truly set you apart."

Polly was as proud as a peacock. She and Miss Purcell were having an animated conversation about the use of different beers in English cuisine. Martha tapped Helen on the shoulder and they both walked toward the doors leading to the car park.

"I'm ready to go. Are we going to Polly's farm to work on tomorrow's plan?" Martha asked.

"Yes, and we need to go soon. Piers and I are having dinner tonight at Healy. Polly says she wants you to stay with her and to bring your pets to her house. She doesn't want your furry family to be left at home. It also gives Pepper a friend or two."

Martha considered the idea. "What about you?"

"She's invited me, as well. I'll drive over after dinner. Polly wants to gossip a bit and told me she thinks of us as the two daughters she never had. By the way, the competition starts at ten tomorrow."

"Sounds good. Let's roll. I'm driving."

Helen flashed Martha a nervous look.

"What?" Martha demanded.

"You've got that certain something about you that says you want to work off some steam. I'm not sure I want to get in the Green Bean (Martha's Mini Cooper) when you have that gleam in your eye."

With her fingers crossed behind her back, Martha answered like she was repeating an honorary code for drivers, "I promise to be a conscientious driver and follow the rules of the road at all times."

Helen narrowed her eyes, not looking unconvinced. "Don't kill us, please?"

Cupping her hands together to form a bowl, Martha replied, " You're in good hands, Helen. Trust me."

"Said the spider to the fly," Helen grumbled but got into the Mini Cooper anyway. She fastened her safety belt and prepared for take-off.

CHAPTER 24

"There's daggers in men's smiles."

-Shakespeare, MacBeth, Act II, Scene III

Detective Inspector Knells sat comfortably in the Chief's office behind the Chief's desk. He liked it here and he'd finished a satisfying phone call with the Chief informing him of his suspension. The old man was furious, but Knells was pleased it was done. The gossips had leaked it to Johns last night. Probably the female constable, Waters, told him. Knells made a mental note to keep an eye on her. Other than that, though, things were going well.

His morning had been informative, as he had gleaned tidbits of personal information about the Chief's life at the Marsden-Lacey Constabulary. One of the more interesting insights into Johns' private world had been his stash of liquor. Knells found it during his detailed sweep of Johns' office. It was hidden inside a woman's black clutch purse and stuffed in the bottom of a fake tree's massive pot. Lots of questions popped up in Knells' mind after unearthing that gem of evidence.

Knells jotted the his thoughts down on a notepad. The hidden liquor would come in handy in the case he was building against Johns. In the last ten years, Knells must have asked himself daily, how he was going to get out of Leeds. He'd considered asking his various supervisors for a relocation opportunity, but in the end, that kind of request was bad for one's career.

If he'd learned one thing all these years working in the police force, it was that getting ahead was political. You had to always look enthusiastic and interested in things the supervising officer liked. This meant, anyone who asked to be relocated was not a team player or had difficulties with authority. It was a no-win situation. The best way to get ahead was to make your own luck. The minute he arrived in Marsden-Lacey, Knells knew he'd hit the jackpot.

The reports were back on the residue samples taken from Mrs. Cuttlebirt's house. It was cyanide, a controlled substance. The killer must have had access to a laboratory or to a not-so-virtuous worker in a laboratory. Since cyanide required about a teaspoon to cause rapid death, someone could have collected minuscule amounts from a lab over time without detection.

Knells had requested Johns' appointment planner and the last six months of cases he'd worked on. If Johns had visited a laboratory, a university with a laboratory, or darkened the doorway of a pharmacy, Knells wanted to know. The one person in Knells' mind who had a real reason to see Saundra Johns dead was Chief Johns. The one person who would have been best at planning her death was also Johns. With time and good detective work, Knells would find the misstep in Merriam Johns' careful execution of his wife's murder.

"Sir?" Sergeant Michael Endicott said, standing in the doorway.

"Endicott isn't it?" Knells asked.

"Yes, sir. It's Endicott. We have all the footage wrapped from the Bake-Off meet and greet. The footage of Saundra Johns at the refreshment table has been enhanced. We think there may be something interesting."

"Good work, Endicott," Knells gushed. "You're going to make an excellent Detective Inspector."

Sergeant Endicott flushed with pleasure at Knells' compliment. "Thank you, sir. I'll send the videos to you. Shouldn't take a minute."

Endicott left the doorway. Knells watched him go down the hallway. The young sergeant's body language effused confidence. Knells would have them eating out of his hand in a week's time. They would want him to be their next Chief.

He turned back to the laptop he was working on and checked his email. There were Endicott's videos. Time to see what he could see, Knells thought to himself. Time to prove Merriam Johns a murderer.

Scene Break

From his pocket, Chief Johns pulled his police badge and studied it. It represented an integral element of his being. The thought of it being gone or taken away was almost horrifying to him. Putting the badge back in the inner left pocket of his suit, he knocked on Donna's door.

A pandemonium of noise erupted within the house. Dogs barking, children's voices yelling 'Mum!', and the sound of a wheeled object rapidly approaching the door made Johns smile and shake his head.

The other side of the door was repeatedly thumped, and a boy was heard saying, "Down Biscuit! Down!" With a great deal of behind-the-scenes work going on, the door finally cracked open to reveal an angelic little face with coal black wispy hair peering up at him.

"You must be Adam," Johns said with a note of fondness in his tone.

The child, with one eye shut against the bright mid-day sun, studied the giant of a man in his doorway. He nodded and replied, as any well-mannered child should, "Yes, sir. Mum is in the kitchen and wants you to come inside. I'll show you," he said proudly.

As Johns squeezed past the partially open door, he realized it was a difficult passage because a toy scooter was blocking it. A substantial, yet friendly Bassett hound sat panting and thumping its tail against the floor in a welcoming beat.

"Follow me!" Adam yelled. Wearing Spider Man pajamas, he jumped onto his scooter and took off down the tiled hallway with Biscuit barking and galloping at his heels.

Their convoy arrived at the back of Donna's house in less than twenty seconds. A soccer game was on the television and two other boys of around nine or ten years of age were lying on the floor over two massive beanbags eating some sort of cracker-filled soup.

"The Sheriff is here," Adam announced threateningly to the other boys who turned around, their eyes growing into saucer shapes at the sight of Johns. They finally found their voices and said, "Hello, sir."

"Hello, lads. Who's winning?" Johns asked, nodding toward the television.

"Manchester!" the boys yelled excitedly. "We're up one."

Johns headed to the comfy chair behind where the boys were lying.

"Hi, Chief," Donna said from behind him, her voice bright at seeing her boss and friend. "Come in here. The kitchen is quieter. We can talk."

A twinge of regret needled Johns at having to leave the room with the dogs, kids and soccer match. He wanted to settle down in the easy chair and soak up the obviously happy domestic environment, plus he would love to see Manchester win today.

"I've got something you're going to love," Donna said enticingly. "I have some of your Mom's winning meat pie from the competition. Polly sent it over. She's such a love. It's absolutely divine. Come have a piece."

Johns perked up a bit at the thought of a piece of Stilton and meat pie. Donna had it sitting on a deep blue pottery plate. She'd poured him a tall glass of cold milk to go with it and excused herself for a minute to grab laundry from the utility room. Johns' mood brightened considerably. He sat down and with a boyish smile, put a fork in the pie.

"Whatcha eating?" came a sweet, frail voice at his elbow.

The Chief turned to see who was moving in on his meal. It was Adam, Johns' earlier superhero greeter. Beside him sat Biscuit, with a knowing look in his dog eyes.

"Lunch?" Johns said, giving the boy a weak smile. The older man knew from the tone of the younger one, that this was a flank attack on his pie.

"Does it taste good?" the child asked, staring intently at the sizable, steaming, crusty piece of heaven on Johns' plate. The Chief saw Biscuit licking his chops in anticipation.

Not having much experience with kids or dogs, Johns, a man over six feet in height and able to bench press three hundred pounds, knew when he was out-classed when it came to real power.

Johns reached down and picked the child up, who didn't hesitate, and put him on his lap. Adam flung his plastic toy light saber on the table.

"If my brother tries to take it," he said looking Johns' directly in the eye, "don't let him, okay?"

Johns nodded, "I'll keep watch."

He handed Adam the fork. Biscuit waddled closer and sat down next to Johns' chair. When Donna came back in, the pie was half gone, Adam had a milk mustache, Biscuit was snoozing across the Chief's feet, and Johns, himself, looked ten years younger.

She put her hand on her hip with a sigh.

"You've been conned by two of the best, Chief. How much has Biscuit eaten of your pie, not to mention, Spider Man here?"

"They've been sharing back and forth. It's about two to one at the moment, I'd say. Adam says it's good pie," Johns said with a warm twinkle in his eye.

"Adam should know. He's already had a piece," Donna gently scolded. "Run out and watch the game with your brother and Jeffery. I need to talk with Chief Johns."

Adam and Biscuit disengaged themselves from their meal train and headed for the living room. Before he turned the corner of the doorway, Donna cleared her throat in a motherly way, reminding Adam he'd forgotten something important. He looked over his shoulder at her questioningly.

"Don't you have something to say to Chief Johns?" she asked, her inflection rising at the end of the question.

Adam made a full front and center turn and saluted the Chief with his light saber while grinning brightly. Using the back of his forearm, he wiped the milk and crumbs from his face. "Thank you for sharing your pie, sir, with Biscuit and me. It was tasty."

Johns nodded and returned the smile. "You're welcome, Adam."

The two well-fed scalawags trotted off into another part of the house with Johns watching them go.

"I'm sorry, they ate your pie," Donna apologized. "Here's another piece. Now, let's talk."

Over the next thirty minutes, Johns learned about Detective Inspector Knells' moving into the Chief's office, requisitioning all the back files on every case Johns had worked on in the last year, and the subtle attitude that he, Knells, was Acting-Chief.

"About an hour ago, Sergeant Endicott sent me the video files from the television cameras. He said to pay close attention to a unique set of video frames," Donna said, opening her laptop and pulling up her email. "What do you think of this?"

Johns studied the video three times. Endicott had done an excellent job of enhancing the visibility. There, in the video, stood Martha and Polly with Saundra as seen from the back. Martha's expression looked like she smelled something bad. Johns surmised Saundra was saying something vicious. Martha reached over and picked up a mug of tea and another, which she handed to Saundra. The rest of the video was a horrific visual of his wife's gruesome death. Closing his eyes, Johns shut the laptop.

"Martha actually drinks out of the cup Saundra gave to the hot water attendant. She hands Saundra her own cup," Donna said excitedly.

Johns nodded. "If it hadn't been that Martha's cup was darker, we wouldn't have ever known the cups had been switched. Has anyone talked with that attendant yet?"

"We think so. It's hard to tell. They came and went all morning and no one actually remembers who handed Martha and Polly their cups."

Johns sat back in his chair and put his napkin next to his plate. "I talked with Dr. Townsend, the Head of Forensics, last night. She must not have known that sharing information with me regarding the case was off limits. The amount in Saundra's body was enough to drop a horse. Someone wanted her dead instantaneously."

"I've been looking into different resources where someone would be able to get their hands on cyanide. All the typical places don't report a loss of any kind," Donna said. The teakettle whined. "Want a nice cuppa, Chief?"

"Yes, thank you." Johns studied the dark beams in Donna's kitchen ceiling. She had different things hanging along them like baskets, dried summer herbs, and antique cooking utensils. "Yesterday I called Saundra's last live-in lover. He didn't answer, but when I told him about Saundra's death, he called me right back. He's in Bombay, not even in England."

"How long has he been there?" Donna asked, pouring water over tea bags in a pretty Ainsley teapot.

"It checked out. He's been there for six months and didn't know anything about Saundra's personal life since they separated."

"Who would want her dead?" Donna mused.

Johns regarded the ceiling again. He smiled. There, along one beam, hung two cornhusk dolls Donna had probably picked up at a summer fair. Whoever had made them had put a great deal of work into them. They each had yarn hair and white aprons. One was a redhead, which made him smile. His gaze locked on the dolls and dropped to Donna.

"I don't think anyone wanted Saundra dead, Donna," Johns said like a man trying to talk underwater. "I think she was handed the wrong mug...the wrong mug. The tea with cyanide was meant for...Martha."

CHAPTER 25

Helen dropped Martha off, along with Amos, Vera, and Gus at Polly's farm and told them she'd be back around eight o'clock that evening. She put the car in drive and turned onto the narrow rural road that would take her around Marsden-Lacey's outer limits and on to Piers' home, Healy House.

The sun was dipping below the horizon making for a glorious sunset over the Yorkshire countryside. The entire day had been beautiful for this time of year, clear and cold, with fast-moving clouds rolling across the vast, blue sky.

Healy's entrance was gated and usually closed. Once Helen knew she was within a mile of it, she called Piers.

"Hi, I'm almost there," she said, when he answered the phone.

"Good, the gates are open. Pull on into the garage area. I'll meet you there in about ten minutes," Piers instructed.

As she pulled through the entrance and onto the blacktopped driveway, Helen looked into her rearview mirror. The massive iron gates were swinging slowly closed. The grounds of Healy were a veritable fortress these days. It hadn't always been so. Since the outrageous situation last fall with the three criminals and the abduction of Emerson, Piers had installed cameras, motion detectors, and hired two security men who patrolled the hundred-acre estate on horseback with dogs. If you wanted into Healy, you needed an invitation.

Helen's Mercedes rounded through the front courtyard area and she drove along a gravel drive to the side of the beautiful Elizabethan house. Toward the back where the stables and garages sat, there was an enclosed outdoor space. Piers stood waiting for her to arrive, looking handsome with his dark hair whipped by the evening wind. He strolled over to her car.

Helen rolled down the window.

"Do you see where the garage doors are open? Pull your car into that bay. It's supposed to snow tonight, and I don't want your car outside," Piers said.

The car parked in the garage, Piers opened the driver's door and helped her out. She smiled up at him through long lashes. As she reached back inside for her purse, he tugged at her free hand, pulling her into his arms. For what felt like an eternity, they kissed. Helen's heart seemed to fill her entire being. She knew she was helplessly in love with him, and there was no going back. It would be what it would be. As she gently pulled back from him, she wondered how it was possible she was both terrified and joyful at the same time.

"Follow me," he said softly taking her by the hand.

They walked through the garages and up a flight of concrete steps into the body of the main house. Healy wasn't a house you walked through in a short time. Patience and fortitude for covering long interior distances were needed by anyone who wished to call it their home.

After reaching a part of the house Helen recognized, they walked down a wainscoted hallway toward the main Hall. Piers opened a tall, heavy mahogany paneled door and waited for Helen to walk through in front of him.

The room she entered was nothing short of magical. Like a jewel, into which one stares deeply to see what lies at its core, this beautiful room was Healy's heart: noble, good and full of grace. No matter where Helen's gaze fell, it was met by something enchanting, something timeless or something loved.

A massive Christmas tree bedecked in glass ornaments and tiny white lights stood regally in front of a diamond-paned, twelve-foot mullioned window. On the room's left, a Gothic stone fireplace played host to a well-stoked roaring fire and a round, intimate dining table dressed for two.

"This is beautiful, Piers," Helen said breathlessly.

Coming up behind her and wrapping his arms around her, he said, "I thought it would be nice, if we had some quiet time, just the two of us. You and I have been running non-stop."

Helen studied the room more attentively. A diminutive silver candelabra sat center stage on the intimate table. Three twinkling candles, along with the glow of the fire, illuminated the Waterford champagne glasses, gold-rimmed Haviland china plates, and two lace-edged napkins. The tablecloth of exquisite ecru-colored damask linen cascaded down into lavish puddles on the floor.

"Come sit down," Piers said, guiding her over to the sofa. Once they were ensconced comfortably, Piers put his arm around her shoulder. Shutting her eyes, she lay her head against his chest and listened to the fire crackle and pop. They sat quietly for some time until a light knock came at the door.

"Come in," Piers said, raising his voice enough to be heard. Both of them rose as the door opened. Agosto, decked out in a black chef's uniform and black skullcap, denoting his high rank among England's culinary guild, wheeled in a cart with a silver domed covered plate.

"Please, Helen, come and be seated," Piers said, holding out her chair for her.

In time, they enjoyed Agosto's pièce de résistance, Hereford Ribeye with seared scallops, and for dessert, flaming mint ice cream. Lingering at the table and sipping champagne, they talked about work, about how Piers' adopted son, Emerson, was liking his new life at Healy, and about how much fun she was having living and working with Martha.

"Agosto is truly an artist. I'm a bit ashamed of our pie today after eating his magnificent meal. If I don't stand up, I may never move again after that ribeye," Helen said, rising and walking over to inspect the Christmas tree better.

Its massive girth was amazing. She tilted her head back to take in the full scope of the tall fir tree and smiled privately to herself. This tree was something out of a child's dream. It soared up into the heavens.

"Come here and sit by me," Piers coaxed from across the room. Helen joined him on the sofa as before. They sat enjoying the fire. He leaned in and kissed her neck. She closed her eyes as the effects of the Champagne, the warm room, and the light touch of his lips on her skin lulled her senses onto a heavenly plane. With a sudden knee-jerk reaction, though, Helen found herself standing up on the floor and looking back at Piers.

"What?" he said, totally befuddled.

"I…I am not sure about this, Piers," she stuttered, looking at him like his head was on fire.

"Not sure about what, Helen? We're two consenting adults. It's pretty natural stuff," he said, his tone tinged with confusion.

Helen walked over to a Wedgwood vase filled with carnations and roses and breathed deeply from them. They filled the air with a heavenly intoxicating scent, making Helen wish that time might stand still, if only for the rest of the evening.

"Piers, I've only ever been with one man. I'm not sure I can go any further. I want to. I really do, but I don't want to be hurt again." She stopped, horrified by her confession, not wanting to look him in the face. "I don't understand why you want...me?"

"Because I love you," he said, his voice rough with emotion. Getting up, he came over to her. "I've spent a lifetime running after everything that didn't matter. I thought I loved Emilia, Emerson's mother, but she never loved me back. I didn't know what love was until I met you, Helen. I didn't know the man I could be until you came into my life. You're making me crazy. I can't work. I can't think about anything, but you. All I want to do is hold you...kiss you."

Helen hadn't expected anything like this from Piers. She stared at him. Without thinking, she blurted out, "I love you, too."

Piers walked with a deliberate stride over to the tree and plucked from one of its boughs an exquisitely petite, black box wrapped with a white silk ribbon. He handed it to her.

"This is for you. Open it," he said softly.

She stared down at the gift. Her fingers trembled as she untied the ribbon. Lifting the box's hinged top, her gaze fell upon the most brilliant diamond ring she'd ever seen in her life.

"It took me three weeks, two trips to Antwerp and a serious scuffle with a love-sick sheikh who wanted that same diamond for his newest wife. Herr Zilberschlag was beside himself trying to appease the sheikh and I both, but once I saw that diamond, I knew it would only ever grace your hand, Helen."

Piers took her hands. "I want you to marry me. Tomorrow would be great. Whatever you want. Make me the happiest man alive. Marry me."

He took it from its pillow and waited for her to look up at him. Her eyes glistening with welling tears, Helen held out her trembling hand for Piers to take. He slipped the ring onto her finger, and she was dazzled by its sheer enormity, as he took her into his arms and kissed her.

"You're mine, Helen, now and for always," he whispered, his words soft next to her ear. "As God is my witness, I'll never let you wonder if you're loved." Piers held her tight. She nodded and said, "Yes, Piers, now and for always."

He took her hand and she followed him. The jewel-like room was left in peaceful silence, while out through the windows, a heavy snow was falling. No one could leave Healy tonight, but then, no one wanted to either.

CHAPTER 26

The next morning, Martha looked out through Polly's kitchen window. Snow clung to the corners of each pane. The farmyard was under at least a foot of snow.

"Helen never made it last night, Martha," Polly was saying as she was heating up water for their morning coffee. "I heard Merriam come home, though. He'll be down for his breakfast."

"We're going to need him to take us in to the competition," Martha said, putting different food items into bags. "Did you decide on which china to use? We should have bought flowers, Polly, before we came home."

"I packed the dishes last night into boxes. Merriam can put it in the Range Rover. We'll be fine driving ourselves. Don't worry about flowers. Look what I have here."

Opening her refrigerator, Polly pulled out a luscious bouquet of yellow and red tea roses, baby's breath and cuttings of holly with round red berries still clinging to the stems.

Martha oohed and ahed over the delicate flowers.

"You never cease to surprise, Polly, m'dear," Martha said giving her hostess a squeeze.

"I am something special, aren't I?" Polly said, sashaying in a silly walk back to the long kitchen work bar. Bending down, she picked up Pepper.

"Would you like some chicken?" she cooed to the tiny dog.

A rattling from the upper story of the house indicated that Johns was about to descend the stairs. Martha checked her hair in the hallway mirror. Polly, oblivious, put four small bowls on the floor filled with minced chicken and gently lowered Pepper to the floor so he could eat.

"Amos! Gus! Vera!" Polly called. "Breakfast!"

Never one to miss out on food, especially a meal involving turkey, bacon or chicken, Amos honed in on her bowl right away and was soon blissfully smacking alongside Pepper. The cats, however, sauntered in with tails aloft and mewed graciously. With refined manners, they ate slowly, with attention to not letting chicken soil their whiskers.

"I'm glad you're here," Johns said, lumbering down the stairs and looking at Martha. "I can't let you continue with the competition, and I'd like it if no one knows that you'll be staying here until we catch the killer."

Both women blinked at him uncomprehendingly. Looking around the room to see if there was someone else her son was speaking to other than her and Martha, Polly finally hesitated a response.

"Who are you talking to, son?"

"I'm talking to Martha," he said matter-of-factly, while taking a mug from the cabinet.

Half-vexed, half-amused, Martha replied, "Is this a weak attempt at morning humor?"

"No. Someone's trying to kill you, not Saundra, not Mrs. Cuttlebirt…you," Johns said, pouring a cup of coffee.

Polly and Martha, both with their mouths slightly open from this shocking statement, didn't speak for a moment. Pulling herself together, Martha asked, "Why would anyone want to kill me? I'm a nice person."

"True, you are a nice person, but someone wants you dead," he said, smiling at her from across the kitchen bar. "You do have a way of working someone's last nerve. Maybe, you've finally annoyed someone to the point of wanting you out of the way."

Johns chuckled at his own joke.

"I don't think you're funny!" Martha exclaimed. "In fact, I think you're being…an ass! I am going to the competition today and you can go to Hell!"

Johns smiled. Martha picked up Amos and stomped upstairs. A door shut firmly somewhere above them.

"What was that all about, Merriam?" Polly demanded.

"I was having some fun with her, Mum, but she's not going to the competition today. You'll need to find a replacement. She's in danger and the only way to handle Martha in these situations is to either lock her up or get her mad."

"How does getting her mad work to your benefit?" Polly asked, while trying to fry eggs and sausages for their breakfast.

Johns put two pieces of toast in the toaster and dug for the butter in the refrigerator. He finally sat down with his coffee and answered her.

"She's up there fussing, stuffing things in a bag, thinking about what I said. It's a distraction until I can handle everything. You see, I'm down here, knowing she doesn't have a car. I'm calling Helen in a few minutes to tell her not to pick Martha up, no matter what, and making sure you are on your way, Mum, without Martha in the car with you. She'll be safe here until I can find out who's trying to kill her."

Johns looked smug and self-assured as he finished. He no sooner took a bite out of his toast than his feel-good expression died as he heard a jaunty triple honk come from the front of the house.

"That woman had better not be doing what I think," he growled loudly as he jumped up to go look out the front window.

"Martha!" he yelled, as he ran outside into the snow with only his stockings on. "Come back here you redheaded…minx!"

His demands would do him no good. She was already down the driveway. He turned and stomped back into the house. Once back in the warm kitchen with sopping wet feet, Johns sat down and removed the dripping socks. Polly smiled serenely as she wrapped up her packing.

"You should have thought that one through a little better, my dear," Johns' mother said, her tone thick with humor.

"How did she do it?" he asked.

Before Polly could hazard an answer, Amos came trotting down the stairs. A big, blue bow was around her neck and a note dangled there with the words 'read me' written on it.

Polly went over and detached the note.

She read:

"Please take care of Amos, Gus and Vera until after the competition today. Tell your son I'm not one of his underlings to dictate his orders to. Also, I lifted your keys from the peg on the way out and used the back stairs. See you in bit, Martha."

"Says here that she snatched the Ranger Rover keys as she stormed out of the kitchen and used the back stairs to go outside. Nice work, if you ask me."

"What time do you need to be at the gymnasium?" he asked quietly fuming at Martha's ability to outwit him.

"Son," Polly began, "you are right about trying to protect Martha. It's more a matter of how you went about it. Don't treat her like she's one of your constables. You were too dictatorial."

Johns sat steaming at the kitchen bar.

"We'll leave in an hour. Should give you time to go stick your head in the snow and cool it down a few degrees," Polly said sweetly. "I'm only telling you this because Martha isn't a woman who will tolerate being talked down to. Now, Merriam, if you would, please put these things in your police vehicle and fill up the wood box for the fire tonight. I'm going to take a long hot shower and doll myself up a bit. Have to look me best. Somebody's going down in this competition, and it's not going to be me!"

Scene break

Martha's cell phone was ringing for the tenth time. She watched it buzz and beep, refusing to take Johns' call.

"Hmph! Someone trying to kill me. What nonsense. I can't think of one person who would want me dead." Then on further consideration, she added, "Not anyone who's not currently in jail anyway."

The phone rang again, but this time, it was Helen. Martha picked up the phone and pressed the 'answer' button.

"Hi," she said grumpily.

"You sound in a jolly mood," Helen said brightly.

"Do you know anyone who would want to kill me? Johns says someone wants me dead and he had the audacity to try and keep me from the Bake-Off Semi-Finals today."

Martha couldn't hear anything on the other end of the connection., "Hey, are you still there or did I lose you?"

"I'm here," Helen answered finally, her early cheerful tone gone and replaced by a more unsure one. "Why don't you clarify for me exactly what he meant by saying that someone wants you dead? Is he referring to a real threat or how you kind of get on people's nerves occasionally?"

"I don't get on peoples' nerves!" Martha exclaimed. "For your information, people generally love me. What is this today: dump on good old Martha day?"

"Simmer down, M. Let's get this conversation back on track. What is going on?"

Martha took a deep breath. She'd pulled the car over to the side of the road to talk legally on the phone. "He says Saundra and Mrs. Cuttlebirt weren't the intended victims. He thinks it's me for some reason."

Neither woman said anything for a short moment. Martha continued, "I shouldn't have left the farm, Helen, but it was like he was telling me, not asking me. I don't like being told what to do."

"Of course, you don't," Helen said sympathetically. "He's forgotten he's not talking to subordinates, but to his… girlfriend?"

"Psshh," Martha hissed. "If he can't remember which is which, I'm not sure he's the right person for me."

"He's having a rough time, too, Martha," Helen remonstrated. "They've put him on suspension, and some new guy is trying to take over at the Constabulary."

Martha pursed her lips. She was feeling bad and ashamed. Johns was probably trying to take care of her, but she wasn't used to being handled.

"I'm turning around, Helen. Do me a favor, please."

"Sure, anything."

"Don't go back to Flower Pot. If someone is trying to…kill me, I don't want you to accidentally get in the way."

"I'm headed for the gymnasium. Whoops, I've got another call coming in. Better go. I'll see you when I see you. Be careful." Helen was gone. Martha turned the car around and called Johns.

"Where are you?" he said without any perfunctory niceties.

"Want to try that again?" Martha said blandly, her temper beginning to rise a bit.

She heard him taking a deep, calming breath. "I am sorry for being too controlling. It's been pointed out to me that you're not one of my officers."

"I should think not!" Martha tossed out.

"You not perfect either," Johns snapped back.

"Close, but…yes, I'm not perfect either."

"You're too hot-headed."

"You're an arrogant mama's boy."

"What the…? Littleword, that's enough. Tossing insults won't get us anywhere."

"Maybe, maybe not. There's some truth, though, in everything we said," Martha said with humor in her voice.

"It's not the most positive way of handling our differences," Johns said.

"I'm bored suddenly," Martha said, her tone blasé.

"Where are you?" Johns said loudly.

"Coming back to the farm. Does Polly need a ride to the competition? I'm on my way there?"

"You've only got yourself to blame, if you're killed," Johns yelled.

"I'll tell you what, Chiefy Poo," Martha blasted back, "if someone tries to take a pot shot at me at the competition, I'll be sure and say with my last dying breath that you were right, and it's my fault I've been killed. Happy?"

Johns clicked the phone off, leaving Martha to consider what a worthy opponent he actually was. Feeling pleasantly contented with herself, Martha turned the car around and headed back to the farm. She was looking forward to seeing Chiefy Poo again. With this last thought, Martha blurted out laughing. If anyone wanted to kill her, it had to be Johns at this very moment.

CHAPTER 27

The competition was in full swing. Harriet's team, Polly's team and The Tea Tarts were all focusing intensely on their creations for the perfect English tea. It had been a grueling two hours and it was coming to a close.

It was interesting to note that many furtive looks were being shot in the direction of The Tea Tart's work area. They were taking a vastly unique approach to the classic tea. In fact, the word 'classic' needed to be tossed out altogether when considering this interpretation. It was more of a national anthem approach.

In the middle of an immense silver trough sat a three-tiered cake on a pedestal dish. The cake had a red icing centerpiece made to look like a fountain. Stuffed all along the sides of the cake were sparklers and British crown memorabilia.

"Crass," Polly muttered under her breath to her team as they worked furiously to apply delicately created icing petals to their cake. "They've lost their minds. Agosto is a Spaniard and Alistair's a proper Brit. Both snobs in their own right. No one wants to eat something that looks like it might blow up in your mouth."

"Teams!" Agosto called over the microphone. "You have one hour!"

If they'd been nervous before, they went into hyper-mode and their movements were frantic. Helen and Martha were busy creating the display for the tea. Each team had been given one round table to decorate. Mr. O'Grady and Polly put tiny real roses and red raspberries as garnish around the too-gorgeous-to-eat chocolate and raspberry cream, layered, torte cake.

"We're done, I think," Helen said, standing back to take in their efforts. "Polly, when you can, please check the table."

"Looks wonderful, girls. Remember when the judges come for their turn at our table, Martha, you and Helen are to be their waiters. Go ahead and get changed. Mr. O'Grady and I are done with the sandwiches, pistachio macarons, chocolate espresso Madeleines, and white chocolate truffles. We only need the scones to come out of the oven."

Helen and Martha walked down to one of the faculty restrooms to get changed. Both were dog-tired from the last three hours of intensity. Finding the room, they went inside.

"I forgot to tell you something, we've been so busy," Helen said. "Would you and Kate consider having Christmas at Healy this year?"

Martha looked up at Helen from inside her button-down Oxford. Wiggling it down over her head, she said, "I guess so. Does that mean you're staying in England?"

"I've invited my daughter, Christine, and her family. Well, to be honest, I invited all three of my children, but only Christine can come. The others have too much going on."

"Are you thinking Christmas Eve or Christmas Day?" Martha asked.

"If you come for Christmas Eve and stay for a few days, it would be wonderful. Healy has so much room and Piers wants people he loves to fill the house. Emerson is terribly excited about Christmas this year."

"You almost sound like the Lady of Healy, Helen," Martha teased, trying to suss out more information from her best friend.

"Well…I think I am…or at least, I'm going to be," Helen said turning around with a huge smile on her face. She'd slipped the ring on and held it out for Martha to see.

"Holy Krakatoa, Helen!" Martha squealed. "That thing is huge! Did he mortgage Healy to pay for it?"

After enveloping Helen in a painful, but joyful hug, Martha asked to see the ring again. "Oh, Helen, you're going to move into Healy. Do you remember our first visit last summer? We said it had something magical about it, didn't we?"

"We did. I remember. It does have something special about it, Martha. I want you there as much as possible. Promise me?"

"Don't you worry, Helen, I'm always going to be Piers' conscience. He better use every available resource at his disposal to treat you well." Martha paused and hugged Helen again, saying, "I know he will, buddy. He's a good guy."

"Do you really think so, M?"

"I do. I really do."

Scene Break

The tension in the gymnasium was at a fevered pitch. Agosto, Lana, Miss Purcell and Alistair were finished with the other two teams and had moved to The Dough Nuts' table. Helen and Martha were serving the tea and answering the judges' questions about the different prepared items. The audience talked in hushed tones, and the television crews discretely performed their camera work.

"Thank you, ladies. Please give us some time to try your cakes and other items. After a short break, we'll announce the two semifinalists," Agosto said with an air of brevity.

The Dough Nuts waited by their workstation, as did the other two teams at theirs. Agosto, Alistair, Lana and Miss Purcell stood up, went over to a long table, and whispered secretly among themselves.

"I don't like the way Agosto looked when he tasted the macaroons," Mr. O'Grady said in a hushed tone.

"He's from Spain. He probably has a feel for pistachio freshness or something," Martha said softly to the other three. They all nodded in worried agreement.

Agosto stood up, and in a regal march to the podium, he mounted the box placed behind it to increase his ability to reach the microphone. He cleared his throat imperiously.

"We have come to an agreement as to who continues on as semifinalists of the Marsden-Lacey First Annual Pudding and Pie Bake-Off."

The audience sent up a nice applause, causing Señor Agosto to lower his head in a dignified acknowledgment of the augustness of the moment. The competitors tried desperately to maintain their composure, but almost everyone was fidgeting in some way or another.

"I would like to say before I make the final announcement that all of our teams showed an exceptionally high degree of culinary expertise and creativity. This decision was difficult and we want to express our profound appreciation for each competitor's participation. Thank you."

"Get on with it, Agosto," Polly muttered, her voice barely audible.

"Our two semifinalists are…Berry's Bakers and…"

The audience went wild with applause, shouts and people standing up calling congratulations to Harriet's team as if they were at a soccer game instead of a cooking contest.

"Please! Please! Quiet!" Agosto, flustered by the uproar, pleaded into the microphone. "We must have quiet!"

Finally, the exuberant audience settled back into their seats and awaited for the last semifinalist to be called. Polly's team and The Tea Tarts' team looked almost miserable from the tension of expectation.

"The last finalist is The Dough Nuts. Congratulations!"

Again, utter pandemonium gripped the audience. People rushed down onto the gym floor. Well-wishers thronged into the cooking areas and happy, as well as not so happy, competitors were congratulated strenuously. Many spectators expressed their excitement for tomorrow's final event, causing the two teams still in the competition momentary stomach knots as they considered that eventuality.

Chief Johns, because he was no longer officially on the police force, had to practically twist Knells' arm to have four officers on hand to watch over The Dough Nuts and, more importantly, Martha. He worked his way through the tight press of humanity using Martha's red hair as a point of reference for his progress.

Finally, he inserted himself into her inner circle of food fans. Seeing him, she called, "We did it!" Flinging her arms up and around his neck, she took Johns off guard and kissed him full on the lips. Any earlier irritation with her was quelled immediately by her exuberance at winning.

"You must be a better cook than I gave you credit for that night when you tried to feed me those skeet pucks," he teased.

"Damn right, I am, Chief," she said wiggling free from his arms and going to re-hug her teammates. She fell in with the crowd and Johns lost sight of her causing him some angst.

The excitement in the room was palpable. The press was interviewing Harriet's team. Agosto was being prepped to do a quick Christmas-interest bit for one of the major news channels. In the blink of an eye, it all changed for Johns. He couldn't find Martha anywhere.

He separated a few well-wishers from Polly and Helen's entourage and asked his mother, "Where did Martha go?" He craned his neck to try to see her, but nothing.

"She's somewhere, probably talking with one of the newspapers," Polly said. She turned back to Mr. O'Grady, who was fielding questions from two flirtatious ladies about his deft handling of the mascarpone tartlets.

Johns pushed through the crowd. Not seeing Martha anywhere, he spoke into his police microphone telling the other officers to locate her, if possible. People were leaving the gymnasium and trickling out into the entrance area. It wasn't in his nature to panic, but something was wrong. He saw her at the same time a woman in the crowd did.

The woman raised her hand to her face and was mouthing the words "Oh my God!" her face a mask of horror. There on the floor was a body and blood was pooling fast.

"Martha!" Johns yelled and ran toward the woman on the floor.

CHAPTER 28

His police training took over. He spoke into his mic telling Sergeant Endicott to call an ambulance. Pushing people away who'd begun to create an encirclement around her, he broke up the crowd to see better. Within seconds, two other officers arrived and moved people from the building. Word of a woman being attacked sped through the crowd like wildfire.

Johns knelt down and turned the woman over. He steeled himself. Shock and relief flooded over him; it wasn't Martha. The woman's eyes blinked. She was breathing.

"I...I," she tried to talk.

"Stay quiet," he said, seeing where the blood was oozing from her lower right side. He took off his sweater, rolled it and put it under her head. "An ambulance is on the way. You're going to be fine."

The woman shook her head and said, "I can't feel any pain."

"That's good. You've been hurt, but you're going to be okay," Johns said, speaking in an even tone, trying to reassure her.

"It was a woman. She came up to me in the gym. The crowd was so tight. I saw her face and something stung me, but..."

The officers had cordoned off the area. The paramedic team bustled into the entry. In less than three minutes, the woman was on a gurney. She was quickly moved out of the building and into the ambulance. Johns watched them leave and, at the same time, saw Detective Inspector Knells glide in through the doors.

"I got here as soon as I could," he said to Johns.

"Did you see the woman's red hair?" Johns asked him without any courtesy in his voice.

"I did, so what?" Knells returned.

"It's the exact same color as Martha Littleword's. Ring any bells in there, Knells?" Johns said, with a tinge of sarcasm and pointing to the detective's head.

Knells wasn't mentally following as quickly as Johns was walking away. He jumped into the Chief's wake, trying to keep up with the powerful man's stride.

"There are three reasons why our two female victims have been killed and this last one nearly killed," Johns said, walking with determination into the gym. "One drank Martha's tea. One lived directly across from Martha's cottage in the only other house on that lane, and this last woman has the exact same hair color."

Johns scanned the room for Martha. "Our killer has missed the mark three times; but have no fear, he won't give up."

Knells didn't say anything but continued to follow Johns, staying in his shadow as they moved through the last few clots of humans.

Both semifinalist teams were at the furthermost end of the gym in the kitchen area huddled around a long table talking to the judges. There in the middle of her teammates stood Martha, completely oblivious to the horrific situation of the stabbing. Johns saw the bunched-up pile of beautiful red hair shift as she moved and shimmer in the sunlight filtering in through the upper-story windows.

His heart took a pause in his chest as if to qualify Johns' own relief at seeing her alive, safe, and (he smiled to himself) smack in the middle of God knows what kind of trouble. Knells came up behind him.

"Your theory may hold water," Knells tried to observe.

Johns turned on him with a searing look of hostility. "Damn right it holds water. Let me get something straight with you, Detective. Getting cozy with the lads in Leeds and having them put me on suspension was pure crap. You know it, too. What's your real game, huh?"

Knells, being slightly shorter than Johns and weighing thirty pounds lighter, stepped back from the angry bull of a man. He shot back, "You're on suspension because you're a prime suspect. That *is* protocol and you know it."

"It's not protocol to sit at my desk, bandy my good name around for a hundred kilometers in any direction of this village, and put your meaty paws on my girl's bum. Why don't you hustle back to the hole you crawled out of, probably someone's arse in Leeds, and let me get back to work finding the real killer?"

Knells lashed back. "I have full authority here, and you *are* on suspension. If you attempt to give me any more grief, you might find yourself more than suspended. How does ex-Chief of Police for Marsden-Lacey sound to you, Johns? I like it here. Your chair feels right."

Johns made a 'hhrumph' sound and stalked off toward the kitchen. Knells turned and walked away toward the front entrance. Neither man would back down. It wasn't in either of their natures. Johns would have to prove his innocence, or the other would have to prove his guilt.

Scene Break

"My hair color?" Martha was saying as she sat slumped in a chair in the corner of the school's kitchen. Helen, Polly, Agosto and Alistair all listened as Johns told them what had happened.

"I think I'm going to be sick, Merriam. You were right and now this woman could be…" Martha said, her face pale. The earlier happiness had seeped out of her spirit. "Oh dear God! I wish it had been me instead of her. I should have listened to you but instead was a hot-headed…Do you know if she's going to be okay?"

"I've got a call in to the hospital. We should know something soon," Johns said. "It's critical, Martha, that you try and consider who might have a reason to want you dead."

She focused intently on her hands lying in her lap and shook her head. "I…I don't know anyone," she said, her manner thoughtful. Squinting her eyes as if inwardly searching for a hiding nugget of insight, Martha was quiet for a moment.

"What if it was someone from when I worked with the law firm?" she said finally. "I only worked in a support position as a paralegal, but it's possible someone may feel resentment toward the firm or even me."

"Did you ever work on any cases where someone was sent to jail?" Helen asked.

"We were a defense firm. Sometimes I would attend court with one of the solicitors representing one of our client's interests. There were times, where fraud or true illegal activity had taken place and it was a part of the indictment," Martha replied.

"I'm going to need to talk with someone at your old law firm, Martha," Johns said. "We need to know if they've had any threats or problems. Also, I'd like a case review. I'll get

Constable Waters to line up photos of everyone involved in cases you were involved in for the last ten years."

"I want to finish the competition, but I understand, if I shouldn't. I don't want anyone else to get hurt. Who can take my place?" she asked the two judges, Agosto, and Alistair.

"How about Perigrine? He's an excellent sous chef," Alistair suggested. "I think he'd be honored, Polly."

"Well, let's give him a call. I'm having my team over to the farm tonight for a briefing on our day tomorrow. You've been a wonderful teammate, and we'll miss you, Martha, but the show must go on," Polly said like a tough military drill sergeant. "Tell Mr. Clark we'd love to have him, Mr. Turner; and if he's interested, to be at my house around six o'clock."

With everyone milling out of the kitchen, only Helen, Piers, Martha and Johns were left. Helen pulled a chair over to where Martha sat.

"What's the best way to keep her safe? Did anyone get a description of the person who…" Helen didn't want to say it because she knew the fear was already working inside Martha's mind. It was like the dream she'd told Helen about only a few days ago and it was becoming a reality, of sorts.

"It's okay, Helen," Martha said, patting her friend on the knee. "I'm thinking about the dream, too. In the dream, it was a woman who tried to stab me."

Johns regarded the women sitting before him with a look of befuddlement on his face. He said slowly, "It was a woman who stabbed our red-headed lady in the entrance hall or someone dressed up like one."

"Merriam, I think this thing has to be played out until the end," Martha said, looking him straight in the eye. "The fastest way to catch this person is to bait the trap. I'm the best bait you've got. Besides, I have a score to settle. Mrs. Cuttlebirt was dear to me. I enjoyed her nosy neighborliness."

"No! No way am I…" Johns stopped before saying another word. He held his breath for a short second and taking a deep breath, he continued, "I'm remembering a conversation you and I had only a few hours ago Littleword."

Martha smiled up at him.

"If I were on board with your bait proposal, what's your plan?" he asked in a co-conspiratorial attitude.

"I don't like the idea at all," Helen exclaimed, jumping up from her chair and shifting her gaze back and forth between Johns and Martha. "She could be killed. That's not a plan!"

"Helen, put your skinny, back-end back down on this chair," Martha ordered gently, pulling Helen down into her chair. "We have to stop this person from hurting anyone else. Merriam's people are going to be stationed all around. Its important, though, to let the press know the woman is alive and give her name. This will draw the killer back out. Whoever it is, thinks they've finished the job already."

"We'll need to get DCI Knells in on this, if we're to have police back-up," Johns said grudgingly. "I'll ask Perigrine, Endicott, Donna Waters, and Sam Berry to help."

"You've got it all figured out," Helen snipped, "but, I don't like it."

"Got to be done, dear. This person has to be stopped. Someone else will get hurt." Martha stood up and dusted the invisible remains of the day from her apron. "Wasn't it Shakespeare, who said delays have dangerous ends? If that be so, then let's give the devil his due."

CHAPTER 29

Sunday at twelve o'clock sharp two terribly determined cooking teams squared off against each other with pudding on their minds. The goal for the last day of competition was for each team to create the perfect traditional English pudding. Not an easy task, especially when you had so many cooks in the kitchen.

Polly's team, The Dough Nuts, was making Lord Randall's Pudding. It was a, chocolate pudding made with heavy brown sugar, apricots and a marmalade topping served with custard. To pull off the dish, they were going to need the full three hours. It was tight, but everyone knew, if done right, it was a true treat for the taste buds.

The opposing team, Berry's Bakers, was also shooting for the gold. They were attempting the Queen of Puddings, or the Monmouth. It was an old-fashioned pudding of baked breadcrumbs in cream, topped with sweet jam, tart berries, and soft meringue.

The tension was at its pinnacle. There was no room for even the tiniest mistake. Time was too precious.

"Here's the marmalade," Helen said, handing Polly the jar. Earlier that fall, Polly had made her own batch of the tangy fruit preserve using Seville oranges. She hoped the infusion of their taste would remind the Spanish Agosto of his homeland and be a mark in their favor.

Their batter was done. They added apricots and the marmalade to the glazed earthen dish. Helen and Martha worked on the custard topping for later.

"Okay, here goes," Polly said, pouring the chocolaty pudding batter over the top of the marmalade. "Let's get the cover made and it'll be time to boil."

With careful hands, they wrapped the top of the basin with parchment and tinfoil tying a string around the rim to create a delicate handle to lower and lift the pudding bowl out of the steaming water. Team Polly held their breath as Mr. O'Grady slowly lowered the dish down into the steamer and put on the lid.

"Start the timer, Martha," Polly said. "We can have a sit, now."

All four of the members of the team looked up at the digital scoreboard on the gymnasium wall to see the timer ticking away. They'd done it and there were two and a half hours left, giving them the perfect amount of time to bring the pudding out of the water, let it sit and be ready for the presentation.

Over at the Monmouth Pudding table, there appeared to be a slight hiccup in the proceedings. One of Harriet's people dropped a dish of raspberries. The pretty crimson berries rolled off in every direction. Polly's team watched the tragedy unfold, actually hoping Harriet had backup bins of berries.

The audience, in hushed whispers, watched anxiously to see how Berry's Bakers would handle the misstep. A frantic search of the coolers and a joyful cry from one of Harriet's team members followed. He triumphantly held up a pint-size bin of raspberries. At least fifty people took a collective sigh of relief at the find.

"They're putting it in the oven," Mr. O'Grady said softly. "They look pretty done in, if you ask me."

"Don't underestimate Harriet," Polly warned. "She's an artist and can handle pressure."

Everyone stood up and milled about. This was the time to chat with the audience and talk to the television crew. Martha had her own entourage: Johns, Donna Waters and Sergeant Endicott.

"How is the woman who was stabbed?" Martha asked.

"She's doing fine, thank God. She was a mother of two teenagers who go to school here," Donna said softly.

Martha, nodding, said, "I'm so relieved she's going to be okay. I'll be glad when this is done today. It's like walking on egg shells. I'm terrified someone's going to get hurt again."

"We checked every purse and bag. The audience was clean and I don't believe the killer is here today," Johns said firmly.

The clock ticked down, and, finally, it was time for the puddings to be put on display for the judges to see and taste. Lana, Alistair, Agosto and Mrs. Purcell discussed among themselves the merits of both entries. Lots of head shaking or nodding by these four caused a high level of nervous tension at the team tables. The judges re-tasted the puddings and wrote down their scores. Agosto tallied the marks.

With a great air of dignity, Agosto scaled the stairs on the gym's stage for the final time. He carried with him a card with the winner's name. More than three hundred sets of eyes watched the card dangle first in his hand, then laid upon the podium, and finally turned up to be read.

"I would like to take the time to ask our audience to please applaud the efforts of these two extraordinary teams."

A wild and enthusiastic applause followed his request with people calling 'good show' and 'bravo'. Agosto raised his hand along with a dignified smile to quiet the highly expectant crowd.

"It is with great pleasure, we give you the first ever recipient of the Marsden-Lacey Pudding and Pie Bake-Off Award: The… Dough Nuts!"

Everyone jumped to their feet, clapping and calling out their congratulations.

Camera's flashed, the television crew moved in for a close-up of Polly, Martha, Helen and Mr. O'Grady hugging each other, even zooming in on a tear or two in the girls' eyes. Harriet came over to Polly and offered her hand, but Polly gave her a strong hug instead. They laughed.

"It's about time you won one, Polly," Harriet chided good-naturedly. "How about helping me at the Bake Shoppe a couple of days a week?"

"Well, my brewing still takes up a good deal of my time and since this competition, I've let my business lag," Polly said graciously.

Martha's protection was constant with Johns, at any given time, only about one foot behind her. Helen came over and said, "We're free to go, but need to be back here for the Christmas parade next Saturday. We're the honorees, so we'll be riding on the Pudding Float. Won't that be a hoot?"

"Are we in the pudding?" Martha asked merrily.

"We're sitting on top of a huge Christmas pudding and are supposed to wear all red. They want us to look like berries or something ludicrous like that," Helen added.

The girls decided to go find Polly and Mr. O'Grady to tell them they were going home. Johns and Sergeant Endicott went with them. Soon, they found their two other team members standing within a group of locals. Mr. O'Grady was carrying the prized pudding. Most of the crowd were the regulars from The Traveller's Inn, Marsden-Lacey's favorite watering hole.

"That's a real beauty of a pudding, O'Grady. You might bring it along to the pub for the celebratory shindig. I can't believe you won," Grimsy, the town gossip/pot-stirrer was saying and shaking his head from side to side. "I'm surprised they let Polly finish the competition."

"Why wouldn't they, Ed?" O'Grady asked. "What have you heard or been saying?"

"Well, Polly's one of the suspects in her daughter-in-law's murder, isn't she?" Grimsy put forward, his eyes twinkling a bit with mischief.

"Why, Polly Johns wouldn't kill anyone or anything and you know it?" Martha said, putting her hands on her hips in a gesture of indignation.

"That's fine coming from you," Grimsy came back, "the other major suspect."

Martha's color warmed. She pursed her lips and walked up to Grimsy, who was about eye level with her.

"I didn't kill Saundra Johns," she said applying emphasis on each word.

Grimsy looked around at the locals who averted their eyes or put their hands in and out of their pockets.

"I'm only saying what everyone else is thinking," he said with honesty. "Both you and Polly had pretty good reasons to snuff her. You wanted Johns for yourself and Polly hated her."

Johns stepped in between Martha, Polly, and Grimsy.

"Ed, I know you're teasing, but you're getting two high tempered women upset with you. Let's all go to The Traveller's and have a pint. It's time for celebrating."

Martha never saw it coming. Right between her and Johns came a brown missile. Somehow, it missed her head and Johns' shoulder to land right in Grimsy's face nearly knocking him off balance with its sheer weight. It dropped to the floor with a thud but left a fairly good-sized chunk of itself behind. Grimsy's tongue came out to lick his lips.

"Pretty good, Polly."

"Nobody calls me a criminal, Ed Grimsy! That goes for the rest of you, too." Polly was like a mad wet hen with her own indignation. "Everybody, look at Ed," she demanded.

The entire group of locals turned to look at Grimsy pulling bits of brown cake from his face and eating it.

"If you really believed Martha or I were poisoners, would you be eating that pudding?" she drilled.

Grimsy continued his ingestion of the yummy dessert.

"Nah, I know you're no murderer, Polly Johns," Grimsy conceded, "but you're a damn fine cook. The proof's in the pudding!"

Everyone burst into laughter and a few slapped Grimsy on the back as they made their way out into the cool winter air. It was time for celebration, good friends and a well-deserved pint at The Traveller's Inn.

CHAPTER 30

Martha, Helen and all three of Martha's four-legged furry people had slept at Polly and Johns' house the previous evening. It had been a rowdy, fun-loving time at The Traveller's Inn and it took Johns driving the three celebrators home to make sure they arrived safely.

Christmas was only a few days away. It was time to bring in the tree. Early that morning, Merriam and Martha went on a short hunt for one before leaving for London to meet with Sinead Peters about Lord Percy's manuscript.

They tramped through the snowy landscape up into the pines and firs along the high ridge. The weather was lovely and cold. In a low pasture below them, a herd of sheep grazed on whatever bits of stubble poked through the snow. A farmer was driving a cart pulled by a tractor with a huge pile of hay for feeding his herd. Like excited children bundled in layers of warm woolens, the sheep ran and mewed at the welcome breakfast.

"My, my, my," Martha said, coming to a standstill to take in the sheer beauty of the Yorkshire countryside. "What a magnificent place to call home."

Johns, too, stopped his climb and surveyed the same valley he'd known as home all his life and that had been in his family for over two hundred years.

"It brings a tear to your eye, doesn't it?" he said simply.

"True, it does. I wish I had arms big enough to reach out and give it a tight hug to myself," Martha said, her arms stretched wide as if to actually give it a try.

Johns laughed at her antics. "You're a funny woman, Littleword. What's your own home like in Arkansas?"

"Different, very different. Deep valleys with dense forests of pine, fir, oak, and walnut trees. Caves of limestone and water, water everywhere. The Osage people called western Arkansas their hunting grounds. We have bears, cougars, coyotes, and lots of snakes, some friendly, some not so friendly."

Johns tried to see the place Martha described as an overlay for the more barren landscape of this part of Yorkshire. "I'd like to go there someday and meet your family."

Martha was quiet. He looked over to her and the earlier radiance wasn't there anymore.

"I said something wrong, didn't I?" he asked.

"After my husband died, my parents came here to live with me to help with Kate. Mama wanted to go home one day. It wasn't much longer that they both passed. I have a brother in Pineville, Missouri. He's a bigwig with an international company in Bentonville. When he's in London, we always go to see him. He likes to take us to tea at the Ritz."

Martha smiled at the memories.

"I still would love to see this place you called home. I've never been to the States."

"It's big, Merriam, so big in some places, it makes your head hurt to try and take it all in," she said thoughtfully. "It's time to take Kate again. She needs to see some things. We're funny pioneers; me and Kate. We're Americans settling in the opposite direction." Martha laughed at her own realization.

Johns watched the red hair play in the wind of the moors and the infectiousness of this Southern lady's spirit warm the otherwise grey day and make it bright.

"I love you, Martha," he said standing there with his tall walking stick looking more like a highland laird than a gentleman policeman-farmer.

Martha smiled up at him, her face rosy from the wind and the walk. "I love you, too." She walked up to him and nuzzled into his warmth, wrapping her arms deep into his open coat and tucking her head under his chin.

"You fit perfectly," he said, his heart beating strongly. Martha could hear it through the layers of clothing and the strong Yorkshire wind.

"Come on, Merriam. Let's go get a Christmas tree. Polly's ready to decorate and we don't want to slow her down."

They headed for the high ground, a place that reminded them both of home.

CHAPTER 31

After the tree was up in its stand and Polly was busy vacuuming up needles, Helen and Martha left for London. They needed to be there by three o'clock that afternoon. All the experts wanted to meet and most were leaving for their Christmas holidays afterwards. The highways were busy with travelers trying to make it home, so the going was tedious.

"So, when we're done," Helen was saying, "let's plan on staying in London for the night. We can do some fun Christmas shopping. I can't believe it. My daughter, your daughter, and all of us will be together at Healy for Christmas this year."

"Ooh, I know. I'm so excited. Could we play hide and seek one night?" Martha asked, her eyes bright with hope.

Helen laughed. "You know what? That does sound fun. Wouldn't Emerson enjoy us playing with him like that?"

"Absolutely he would. Children love it when adults play kid games. More adults should try hide and seek. A house like Healy was made for the game."

Nodding, Helen said, "You're definitely right. Let's do it."

Martha sat back with a contented smile on her face.

"Of course staying in London tonight is exciting, too. I want to go somewhere tomorrow to pick out some things I know Kate wants."

Soon the girls were in the great city of Westminster Abbey, Big Ben, Sherlock Holmes, and Harrods. They parked the car and went to the offices of Hisox Insurers.

Sinead Peters, a pretty, blonde Irish woman of about thirty-five, met them in the glass and steel modern lobby. She shook both their hands.

"Follow me, ladies. Almost everyone is here. We're waiting on Sir Alec Barstow. He's coming down from Cambridge."

They stepped into a glass-cage elevator and were whisked downwards. When the doors opened, they were, at least, three stories below ground level. A security guard wearing a semi-automatic gun in a side holster gave a curt nod as Sinead ran a retinal scan on her right eye. Clicking noises were heard as the computer verified her identity, followed by the sound of heavy metal bars moving inside the vault door. Sinead pushed the surface with only her fingertips, and the door opened to her touch.

"Wait for me," a baritone voice boomed behind them. "I'm not as quick on my feet as even yesterday."

It was Sir Barstow, the scholar from Cambridge. He was, at least, eighty years old, a bit hunched over from years of assiduous study, and wearing a huge, padded Skipsea jacket with toggles for buttons. His smile was cheerful and his color ruddy.

"Nice to see you again, Helen," he said with warmth in his voice. "You look beautiful as always."

Helen gave him a hug and a kiss on his cheek, making his eyes shine even bluer. "And you are more charming each time I see you, Alec," she returned.

"Who's this?" he said, turning to Martha with almost a roguish tone and a sparkle to his expression. "I know I would have remembered meeting you, my dear," he said to Martha, who extended her hand for him to shake. He accepted it more as a gallant than as a business colleague, and, lifting it to his lips, he kissed the top of it with a gracefulness honed from years of experience charming women.

Martha was delighted. She beamed up into his wise, yet sprightly face and actually blushed.

"My name is Martha Littleword. I'm Helen's new colleague."

"Well, allow me to let you in on something," he said, lowering his voice and bending down closer in order to achieve a more confidential position. "In a minute, a bunch of puffed-up academics and literary experts, not to mention a doctor in forensic analysis, will begin sniffing over that manuscript. The scientist won't care if it's authentic or not, he's a numbers man, but the others have a lot riding on their interpretation, mainly their entire careers. I'll know if it's legitimate in less than ten seconds. Blow them all out of the water."

He pumped his eyebrows up and down, smiling mischievously.

Martha grinned with sheer enjoyment of this man's force of personality. "How will you know it's the real deal?"

He laid his finger aside his nose and winked at her. "I'm a divvy, darling. Have been since I put my hands on my first Gutenberg bible. It's a tingling and quiet awe you feel when you touch something. The item speaks to you in a way fiddle-faddle stuff never will. Your senses come alive and you are humbled. Helen has a bit of the divvy in her as well."

"How do you feel about a little wager? We could put some money down on how long it takes for the experts to make a decision," Martha whispered to her new favorite.

Barstow gave her an appraising look.

"I like the way you think, Red. You're on. The loser has to buy the winner dinner. I say they poo-poo it on the first go-round, then white-coat over there will talk about DNA tests and some such stuff, which will cause them all to reconfigure their assessments. If it hasn't already occurred to them, they'll actually start looking at the manuscript. The whole process, with tea break, will take at least two hours. Tiresome stuff."

Martha looked around the room at the collection of men and women. Sir Barstow might be a divvy when it came to documents, but Martha Littleword was a divvy of the human animal. She smelled the anticipation and excitement in the air of the room. Too many furtive glances at the simple manuscript lying on a white cotton sheet in the middle of a table told her those experts were itching to get their hands on it.

"I tell you what, Sir Barstow," she said quietly, still maintaining their confidential attitude, "I say it only takes forty-five minutes after the reading of the forensic report for them to call it a draw. They're going to want to reconvene at a later date in order to check their sources."

The old, wizened scholar laughed uproariously, causing the others in the room to almost jump out of their three-piece suits and shoot affronted looks in their direction.

"If I've been in one of these academic poker matches, I've been in a hundred. I like my steak and lobster from Goodman's in Soho. Wear something plunging and black."

With one last wink, he sauntered over to the table and chatted with the other people. Martha couldn't help adoring him. He was a caution, as her grandmother would have said.

Sinead Peters started the meeting and soon Helen joined Martha over on the modern looking grey settee next to the wall.

"It's going nicely. No one is contesting anything. I bet we know something in a preliminary sort of way, in less than an hour," Helen confided quietly.

"Who's the heavy?" Martha asked.

"The heavy? What do you mean?"

"You know, the one the rest of them will, at some point, finally fall in line behind?" Martha explained.

"Oh, yes. Well, that would be the other white-haired man wearing the red bow tie, checkered shirt, and white tennis shoes."

"The one who looks like he's swimming in his own clothes?" Martha said, with a low chuckle.

"Yes, that's the one. He's the scholarly antithesis of Sir Barstow. Barstow's a divvy and the best in the world, whereas Dr. Edmond Winters has a Phd in Tudor Theatrical Studies, written six books on Shakespeare's life and work, and authenticated Elizabethan works on paper for almost every major museum in both hemispheres."

"So, if Barstow says it's Shakespeare and Winters says it isn't, what happens?" Martha asked.

"It's hard to say. The forensics have come back and the man wearing the grey suit, Dr. Eisner, says all the tests are spot on for the early seventeenth century. Handwriting analysis was done, as well. They compared the manuscript with the only known examples of Shakespeare's handwriting, which are his signature. It's going to be interesting."

Suddenly, a brouhaha erupted at the table. Sir Barstow and Dr. Winters were arguing with a lady in a navy suit, Dr. Barbara Penrith, from Nottingham.

"It's impossible to say if Shakespeare, Dr. Winters, was familiar with a cat named Minerva. The point is, he usually used cats as a metaphorical tool, but in this instance, he gives the cat a proper name. I don't see this being his work at all."

"Rubbish!" Sir Barstow exclaimed, pounding his fist on the table causing everyone to jump in the room. "'There are more things in heaven and earth, Barbara, than are dreamt of in your philosophy.'"

"I have to agree, Barbara," Dr. Winters joined in. "Your argument is sound in that cats have been used in a negative light in all of Shakespeare's plays, but that does not preclude his possible use of them in a positive one. Besides, it's well known that he was fond of his publisher, Edward Blount, who loved cats. It's possible Shakespeare may have put the cat in as a way of paying homage to his friend."

"Why, that's right, Edmond," Sir Barstow said, snuggling up to his usual nemesis with a newfound love. "There's also precedence for the unusual use of the dog, Crab, in Two Gentlemen from Verona. If we're going to get sticky about it, Barbara, we need to rekindle the age-old squabble about how Shakespeare was able to write so convincingly well about Italy having never visited there. The cat is not an issue. Am I right, Ed?"

Sir Barstow and Dr. Winters had never been on the same side before. It caught them both off guard and poor Dr. Penrith was casting around the room for some form of formal support.

"Okay, okay," she said. "I'll consider ceding on the point regarding the highly unusual characterization of a cat, but we need more time to consider the text. Certainly, parts of this play have Shakespeare's voice, but it will take time to compare this manuscript with other earlier known examples of his plays."

Helen stood up and went over to the table. "So, should we push for a second meeting?" she asked enthusiastically.

"Absolutely, and have the people from Sotheby's and Christie's here. We need them to try and imagine an unfathomable amount this priceless thing may be worth," Barstow crowed flinging his hands above his head.

Everyone laughed and soon they all made their way to the elevator. The meeting had been almost exactly fifty minutes in total. Martha and Helen walked out with Sir Barstow and Sinead Peters, taking the lift together.

"What time is dinner?" Martha said, giving Sir Barstow a few mischievous bats of her eyes.

The well-read rapscallion nudged up against her. "You are a devilish woman, and I'm completely at you and my lady Helen's service. I'll have my car pick you up at seven. Please tell me you're not married." With a scandalous smile, he exited the glass elevator and lolloped toward the exit saying, "Don't forget, something plunging!"

"Phew," Sinead said, once they saw him hopping into the back of his Rolls, "he must have been quite the Romeo in his time."

"I'd say, he's still playing the game. Probably not doing too badly, either," Martha observed.

"One thing's for sure," Helen said, turning to the two other women, "we've had an incredible success. Let's get to the hotel, have a glass of champagne and wait for Sir Barstow's chauffeur to arrive. Something tells me, we're dining in style tonight."

CHAPTER 32

The car stopped in front of the hotel and Helen and Martha, tired from their long day, took their luggage and went inside to the reception desk, letting the steward take their car to the garage. They checked in and went to their room immediately.

"I'm going to lie down and sleep for an hour. Sir Barstow's message said he won't pick us up until seven thirty," Helen said, plopping down onto the fluffy white linen duvet and sinking deep into its pillowy softness with a sigh.

"Me, too," Martha said, already tucked in between her sheets. "I'm beat. That gives us, at least, an hour to nap."

"I talked with Mr. Brickstone. He's extremely happy and told me to enjoy London." Helen's voice trailed off into soft breathing. The girls slept.

They must have been asleep an hour because when Martha awoke, the room was dark and the only light coming in through the curtains were the street lamps and other city lights. Helen was still curled up like a contented baby, so Martha went into the cozy sitting room adjacent to their bedroom. Shutting the door to not wake Helen, she grabbed her phone and checked the time. There was a message from Mr. Brickstone. He had asked for her to call him at her convenience.

No time like the present, Martha thought to herself, so she dialed the number.

"Hello, Mrs. Littleword. Thank you for calling," he said pleasantly.

"Hello, Mr. Brickstone. I saw your message. How may I help you?"

"I sent another document by carrier to your hotel. Helen's not answering her phone and I'm nervous about having it left at reception. I wanted to let you know it was there and hoped you'd retrieve it."

"Yes, Helen's taking a rest. It's been an exciting day. I'll run down and get it for you. Please don't worry. I'll make sure she gets it."

Mr. Brickstone thanked her and hung up. Putting on her shoes, she left a note for Helen on the coffee table and grabbed her phone. Outside in the hall, Martha realized she didn't have any pockets, so she stuck the phone in her bra along with her room card and went down to the lobby.

Martha checked with the front desk clerk. There weren't any packages for Mrs. Ryes. He asked her to give him a moment to check with one of the other attendants. Martha agreed and went into the traditional English sitting area. She sat down in a wine-colored leather wingback chair near the fire to wait.

"Mrs. Littleword," a timid female voice said behind her. Looking around, Martha saw a young woman standing beside her chair.

"Yes?"

"My name is Melissa Sutherland. I'm sorry to be late. The weather is turning bad and I had a nervous drive from Warwickshire."

"That's okay, Miss Sutherland. I hope you're not going to try and go back again tonight," Martha said kindly.

"Yes, I have to. I'm the nurse for Lord Percy Farthingay."

Martha remembered Denise saying that the Lord had a nurse. "I talked with Mr. Brickstone only a few minutes ago, are you the carrier with the package for Helen?"

Melissa nodded. "Oh no! The package is in the car. What was I thinking?" She dug in her purse. "It's all the way back in the car park."

"Come on. I'll walk with you. Is it the hotel's car park, because I didn't bring a jacket?"

"Yes, thank you. I don't know where my head is," Melissa said.

They found the hotel exit to the car park and walked through the long cement underground hall.

Melissa pointed. "It's over there, the black sedan."

Together they walked over to the car. The entire place was quiet.

"I'm so afraid it would get a dent. It's not mine, but Mr. Brickstone's," she said.

"Hey! Martha!"

Martha and Melissa spun around to see Helen coming through the heavy metal doors of the parking garage.

"Hi!" Martha called. "Did you find my note?"

Helen caught up with them, a bit out of breath.

"Well, I saw the note and was worried, so I ran down and the porter said you left with a woman heading to the car park."

"Mr. Brickstone called and needed to get a package to you. Miss Sutherland," Martha indicated the woman, "brought it all the way from Warwickshire this evening. She forgot it in the car."

Martha smiled congenially at Helen, who had an odd expression on her face. It resembled someone who'd been shown something terrifying. Martha's eyes followed the trajectory of Helen's stare, to find Melissa holding a gun on them both.

"Get in," she demanded. "Both of you."

Scene Break

The light of day was beginning to ebb as the sun slipped behind the tall, stately pines of Greenwoods' hills, leaving purple and crimson streaks of color across layered clouds. Mrs. Norton, the cook at Greenwoods, scrubbed the wooden kitchen table with a vigor that testified to her troubled mind.

All day something had been worrying her. It started the moment she awoke. It was a sense of urgency and it had increased with each hour as she'd gone about her work, trying to ignore it. Denise's entrance into the kitchen, interrupted Mrs. Norton's thoughts.

The young woman went over to the sink and taking a glass from the shelf, she poured water and drank deeply.

"Nellie," she said, "I've had my wits scared out of me."

Mrs. Norton, but called Nellie by Denise, took in the girl's face. Noting the lack of color in Denise's normally rosy cheeks, the older woman laid down her scrub brush.

"Denise, come have a sit-down and I'll make you some tea. That'll fix you up nicely. You can tell me what happened."

Nellie was the mother of three hardy Yorkshire farming men, now all in their thirties and with families of their own. She'd taken this job as a way to have extra money for her grandchildren, all boys as well, but it was in her nature to mother, even when a young person like Denise, wasn't of her own making.

"I've had a troubled spirit all day, m'self, lass. I keep turning around half expecting to see something or someone. Tell me what happened."

When the tea was ready, they sat by the warm Aga stove propping their feet against some old iron doorstops so as to feel the heat better.

"I was supposed to carry boxes Mr. Brickstone wanted moved out to the front entrance. I'd put them all on the dolly and was almost to the place in the hall where the huge family crest hangs over the banister. I looked up and there was this beautiful lady standing there."

Denise's face mirrored what it must have looked like at that moment of seeing the woman. Her eyes were wide, uncomprehending, and her mouth slightly ajar.

"Did you speak to her?" Nellie asked, sitting a bit more upright.

"I did. I said, 'May I help you.' She shook her head without speaking and turned to walk out the main doors. I watched her go down the stairs and stop. She turned around, and I swear, Nellie, she wanted me to follow her."

"Oh, Denise, what did you do?"

Denise swallowed a sip of tea. "I wasn't afraid, Nellie. She didn't scare me at all. The room smelled of lavender. I walked out to the top of the entry steps. She'd already somehow made it to the long lane surrounded by pines that leads to the main gates." Denise took another sip. "She was looking at me from there and I started down the steps, and she smiled, turning again to walk through the pines."

"Did you feel like you needed to follow her?"

"Yes, more so than ever. I tell you, Nellie, it was like she wanted me to leave the house. I stopped because I knew Mr. Brickstone would be back and I needed to finish my work, so I turned and returned to the front doors. Something, curiosity perhaps, made me turn and look for her. She was there, but her face was sad. That's when the wind came through, and I tell you, Nellie, she disappeared. Gone."

Nellie sat back in her chair and scanned the room. Shadows were settling in different corners and the house was entirely too extensive, too empty, and too lonely. Her own feelings all day were of dread.

"Denise," she said putting down her teacup. "I want you to go and pack all your things."

The young woman started to object or question the older one's decision, but she only managed a, "Why?"

"I'll tell you when we're in the car. Hurry! Go on. I want to leave in a quarter hour."

Denise asked, "Are you going to leave, no matter what?"

"I am."

"Okay," she said, her mouth pursed to one side in a contemplative expression. "I'll be right back."

Nellie went to her own room and threw her things into a few suitcases then returned to the kitchen to wait. She remembered the last time she'd felt this way. It was the last time she saw her husband. Death came that day, and if she was right, it had been skulking about all day today, as well. Nellie would rather error on the side of safety, especially considering her responsibility to Denise, than worry if people called her a looney old woman.

Waiting on Denise, Nellie put the last teacup away. She unconsciously raised her eyes to look out the windows over the sink. What she saw there made her drop the fragile china cup into the sink where it broke in two. Her eyes never moved from the form of a woman in a long black dress standing at the far garden wall staring at her with sad, pleading eyes.

Nellie understood instantly that her course of action was correct. She pulled her gaze away from the specter and collected the broken cup from the sink throwing it in the dustbin.

"Denise! Denise!" she called.

Rapid footsteps echoed down the hall as agile feet hurried toward her.

"What is it?" Denise arrived through the darkness, holding her case and panting lightly.

"Let's go. I want to get you home."

Denise's eyes were round and wide with questioning, but she obeyed Nellie and they walked together out of the house. Within less than five minutes, Nellie's car's tires crunched on Greenwoods' gravel as she maneuvered it down the long drive. It was with a sigh of relief, they passed through the entrance gates and increased their speed toward home leaving Greenwoods to itself and to its lady.

CHAPTER 33

The black Mercedes limousine threaded its way through the holiday nighttime traffic. In the car's back seat, Helen and Martha sat in extreme discomfort while Brickstone kept a handgun leveled at them. He appeared annoyed by the circumstances in which he found himself. His mouth curled into a thinking expression.

Never taking his eyes off them, he asked Melissa, "What went wrong? We didn't want Ryes. You screwed this up, Mel. Now I've got to kill two more."

Neither Helen nor Martha talked. They listened to Brickstone berate Melissa about letting him down. Occasionally, the young woman would blubber something about doing exactly what he'd told her to do. Martha watched the man closely and slowly her memory worked at the puzzle of who he was.

Brickstone noticed Martha's scrutiny. He sighed and wagged the gun as he said, "You must be wondering how we know each other, Mrs. Littleword."

"Yes," Martha said slowly, looking at his face, watching his mannerisms and his…birthmark! Her sudden recognition showed in her expression.

"Figured it out, did you?" he said, the gun barrel tapping lightly on the car seat as he leaned over. "I knew you would. It was only a matter of time. The real pity is how pitiful a killer I've turned out to be. I mean really, three hits and three misses. Not my specialty. My talents lie in pursuing and procuring valuable commodities."

"There's another less pretentious way of putting it," Helen asserted. "Fraud and thievery."

Martha reached over and applied a gentle warning pressure to Helen's arm. "He's got a gun, so he gets to talk."

Helen rolled her eyes and mumbled something about another lunatic in her line of work.

Brickstone, like any megalomaniac cutthroat, was finding that his captive audience elevated his desire to delve into his raison d'être.

"All the death, all the killing, it had to be done. If Mrs. Littleword recognized me, she'd blow my sweet situation. Playing the future laird of the estate has been absolutely delicious. I've made a tidy sum from the sale of things from Greenwoods. There's an island with my name on it not far from St. Martin."

"So you're not Lord Percy's nephew?" Martha asked.

"No. He lives in Auckland, New Zealand."

"Where is Lord Percy?" she asked.

"He died. Didn't he, Melissa?" Brickstone asked of the woman driving.

"He did, Ricky. He died in his sleep. Went quiet like an angel, not a peep out of him."

"See. I didn't have anything against old Farthingay, I only needed Mrs. Littleword's silence. She had the potential to remember me at any minute. It was pure bad luck, you showing up with Mrs. Ryes that day. Pure bad luck."

"More for my neighbor Mrs. Cuttlebirt, Saundra Johns and some poor woman I don't even know who has hair like me," Martha pointed out.

Brickstone waved the gun. "Better calm yourselves, ladies. I don't want to have to use this in the car. I love this car." He wrinkled his nose. "Could get messy and unnerve my driver. I need her to get us back to Greenwoods. I have to figure out what to do with you both. I've got too many women cluttering up my life at the moment."

He yawned. "Rather tired of all this slinking about. So, who would you recommend to manage the sale once you're gone?" he asked Helen.

"Rot in Hell," Helen muttered.

"I don't want to kill you, Mrs. Ryes. I need you to sell my manuscript. I guess I'll have to give Sinead Peters a ring." Brickstone sighed in a long drawn out martyred way. "You American's, your veneer of politeness is so thin. Such an aggressive culture." He turned around and a glass divider slowly rolled up between the seats.

"Melissa, let's get to Greenwoods. I'm utterly exhausted. I think the old limekiln will be a nice holding place. Hasn't been used in half a century probably."

CHAPTER 34

"When shall we three meet again? In thunder, lightning, or in rain? When the hurly-burly 's done, When the battle's lost and won."

-Shakespeare, MacBeth, Act I, Scene I

Brickstone stared gloomily into the blazing fire. He knew his situation was crumbling around him. The minute he'd realized Melissa's colossal mistake and what it would cost him, he'd decided to rid himself of all his loose female threads. But what did he find, when he'd got home? Two of those threads had already slipped the noose. It was extremely possible Mrs. Norton and Denise sensed something was wrong, once Lord Percy was gone.

He stalked around the library. Picking up another log from the pile, he tossed it onto the fire, watching it catch flame and burn. A smile played about his mouth.

"Melissa!" he bellowed, "Melissa!"

He'd make her start the fire in the kiln, put her hands on the shovel to fill the furnace, and make her light the match. When the authorities came sniffing around, he'd be long gone, and they'd find three sets of human bones and not an ounce of evidence to ever pin anything on him.

Scene Break

She'd packed her things neatly in a suitcase. Her mind was free to chew on the horror of the last few hours. Melissa walked over to the wall mirror hanging in her bedroom and forced herself to look. The reflection of who she might become terrified her. Every fiber of her body told her to run. Ricky was mad. She knew it for certain, and if he intended to kill the two women, she wasn't having any part of it.

Leaving the bag behind, she gently let herself out of the room and down the back set of stairs. The key to the tiny door of the kiln was hopefully still on the bureau in the front hall where Ricky left it after locking the women in. Melissa restrained her breathing and made an intense effort to keep quiet as she passed the long hall leading down to the library where Ricky was brooding.

"Melissa! Melissa!" his call froze her in mid-stride, sending the hairs on the back of her neck and arms into upright positions. She willed herself to move. The key was only another fifty feet away. A door slammed somewhere in the darkness. Melissa's fear propelled her to move in haste. She found the key and thanked Heaven above that it was still where they'd left it.

Slipping out into the night, Ricky Brickstone's last hope and alibi fled down the front stairs of Greenwoods and down the path toward the old kiln.

Scene Break

The first thing Martha became aware of was the cold and the smell of damp. She squeezed her eyes shut, hoping the pressure would push the other sensations away. Nothing, so she opened her eyes. Instantly, she shut them again. Her mind temporarily shot into a panic. Sitting up, she took in her environment. A room made out of stone, with no windows and only one door. The light of the full moon shown down illuminating the space in a cold light. Her nightmare made real.

She'd lay on the floor wrapped in a blanket. Her head hurt terribly. Another body, warm beside her made a groaning sound. Helen came to life beside her. Martha shook her until she roused herself completely.

"What happened?" Helen sat up, her hair askew and her face smudged with some kind of gunk.

In an effort to make her mind think straight, Martha rubbed her temples.

"The last thing I remember was getting out of the car and listening to Brickstone whine about finding a vacuum to get rid of any evidence in his car."

"That's right," Helen said groggily. "He was in the car and Melissa... They had a needle! Remember?"

"Yes, I remember." Martha looked around.

Helen stood up and brushed herself off. She was still wearing the yoga pants she'd put on to take a nap in at the hotel.

"It's freezing in here. Where are we?" she said, rubbing her arms to make them warm.

Martha saw a wooden lid about fifteen feet above her. She must have been asleep for hours, but it was dark, no light filtered down through the cracks in the lid.

"I think they dragged us in here and by the looks of you, they may have used your hair to pull you," Martha said, handing Helen the blanket to wrap herself in.

Helen patted her hair with both hands. I feel like I'm covered in soot. It's all over our faces and clothing. Taking the blanket, she wrapped it around her. "Thanks, can we share?"

"Helen, didn't he say something about a limekiln in the car?"

Standing up, Martha waved off the offer of sharing the blanket.

"He did, and if I remember correctly, he didn't know what to do with us. There's a door; let's try it."

Helen got up and went to try to turn the ancient iron handle. Only the sound of rubbing metal on metal replied to the effort.

The door didn't budge. Turning around, she moved her hands along the kiln's wall, looking for a key.

"Maybe there'll be a key hidden," Helen said. "Ugh!"

"What's wrong?" Martha asked, her voice worried.

"Something big is lying against this wall in this shadow."

Martha went to Helen and knelt down gingerly touching the large mass on the floor.

"Oh, my God! Helen, it's a body in a bag!"

Both women jerked back at the revelation.

The women moved back to the other side of the kiln's space. The realization that this was her nightmare come to life, crept into her consciousness and stung at the back of Martha's mind. She pushed the idea down, locking it tightly within a mental cryptex. It wouldn't do to panic.

Suddenly, her right breast buzzed as if something was alive within her bra. Immediately, she panicked thinking it might be an insect that had crawled into her clothing while she slept on the floor. Frantic with the image of a spider somewhere within her shirt, she pulled at her shirt.

"What's wrong?" Helen demanded.

"It's a bug in my shirt!"

"Yuck! Come here, I'll help you."

Martha, digging down between her breasts, realized with a thrill of joy, it was her phone buzzing her, not a bug. She pulled it free, remembering how she'd stuffed it there earlier at the hotel. Merriam was calling. She tapped the button.

"Merriam!"

"Martha! Thank God! You finally answered. Where are you?" he was practically yelling into the phone.

"I…I…don't know. We are in some kind of stone pit. It's freezing."

"We've been trying to trace your phone. Are you…." Johns was saying, but he was gone.

"Merriam? Merriam, can you hear me?" Martha called into the phone, but nothing. She looked down and saw the energy level at the top of the screen showing only one bar.

"I can't believe you had your phone on you this entire time," Helen marveled.

"We are so lucky it didn't buzz while we were in the car with Brickstone. I'm going to try and call Merriam again. We've got to tell him where we are."

She tenderly held the phone as if it might perform better if she were patient and sensitive to its needs. Helen pressed close to lend support to Martha's ministrations upon the phone. Dialing Merriam's number, they barely breathed, in hopes it would go through.

He answered. "Merriam we're in the old limekiln at Greenwoods in Warwickshire," Martha blurted as fast as possible into the speaker.

An expectancy hung in the air. Had he heard her?

"Martha? Did you say Greenwoods?" came his voice.

Both women immediately huddled closer and with great urgency, Martha answered, "Yes, Merriam. Greenwoods in an old lime pit. Can you hear me?"

The phone made a bell sound and a message blipped up on the screen saying 'low battery'. They looked at each other with dread.

"Do you think he got it, Martha?"

"If he did, I know he'll be here within the hour, but we've got to help ourselves, too."

"Okay, but Brickstone will probably have a gun."

"We need a plan."

A scraping sound above them made Helen and Martha move to the side of the kiln below a stone overhang to hide. They peered upwards. Soon a woman's head appeared. It was Melissa.

"Hey! Are you okay?" she called down to them in a low voice.

Martha and Helen exchanged unsure looks. Neither uttered a sound.

"Hey! I want to help you," Melissa said with an urgency in her voice.

Helen poked her head out. "We need to get out of here, Melissa. We can help you, too, if you'll let us."

"Do you see a door with an iron handle?" she asked in almost a whispered cry.

"Yes, we see it," Martha, stepping out from her hiding place, said. "Can we get out through it?"

Melissa threw something down. It clinked as it hit the stone floor. "That's the key. Use it quickly and crawl out. He plans to…" she stopped her words. "Just hurry!"

The head disappeared from the circle above them and the wooden cover was pushed back in place. Helen and Martha dropped to their knees and felt around on the floor for the key.

"I've got it!" Helen jubilantly cried. Standing up, she helped Martha to her feet. "Come on, let's give it a try."

Using their fingers, they felt for the tiny place to insert the key and found it.

"Go slow, Helen. It might be fragile and break, if we turn too hard," Martha warned.

With a tenderness reserved for taking test samples from delicate, priceless documents, Helen worked the key into its lock and ever so gently turned it. The mechanism gave and the door swung open.

Martha stopped Helen from going immediately through the child-size aperture. She pulled Helen close and whispered into her ear, "What if it's a trick? We need to go slow and listen."

Helen nodded, and Martha picked up one of the hand-sized stones that lay on the kiln's floor and gestured for Helen to follow her. They knelt down, and squinting her eyes into the darkness, Martha crawled first into the hole.

"What do you see?" Helen asked, following Martha into the blackness.

"They must have pulled us or shoved us through here. Hey! I see light! Come on, Helen. We're almost out."

The girls crawled for about five feet and exited into a shed.

"This must be where they prepped the kiln. Look! There's lots of wood and charcoal stacked up," Martha said pointing to a hefty pile of burnable kindling.

"Oh, my God! Martha! He was going to start a fire!" Helen hissed.

Holding up a rope, Martha announced, "I've got an idea!"

CHAPTER 35

Johns' phone was ringing. Sergeant Endicott maneuvered the car easily back and forth between drivers on the highway. They'd covered the usual two-hour drive in less than an hour and twenty minutes. It was the police chief of the village outside Greenwoods, Johns answered immediately.

"Bennie."

A man's voice said, "I'm sorry Johns, but our hands are tied. Your supervisor says you're on probation and not to assist you. If I help you, I'm asking for a substantial fine."

Chief Johns held the phone away from his ear. His anger stoked once again by Knells' ridiculous accusations. He mastered his emotions and replied, "Bennie, do me a favor. If you can get away in about an hour, meet me at the entrance gates. Consider this more of a social call than a professional one."

"I'm there. By the way, Merriam, that Knells is a real piece of work. One of my constables worked in Leeds about five years ago, Knells doesn't like team sports. He's a snake."

"Thanks, Bennie. I'll see you in an hour."

Johns turned off his phone.

"Sir?" Endicott began.

"Yeah, Michael."

The young sergeant took a deep breath, and as if he was ready to say something he didn't relish, he banged the steering wheel with his hand.

"What is it, lad?" Johns asked, a bit stupefied by his sergeant's unusual emotional outburst.

"Knells has asked each of us to write a statement regarding your conduct. He said if we didn't acknowledge your…"

"Spit it out, lad. I'm fully expecting that louse to manipulate my team to win himself my position as Chief," Johns said with disgust in his voice.

"He wants us to acknowledge your affection for a nip or two while on duty." Endicott let out a gust of air from his lungs. "There I said it, but, sir? We all know about the black purse in the tree pot, and when he found it, we all tried to play dumb. He told us if we didn't talk, we'd be written up. We need these jobs, sir."

Endicott hung his head slightly, whereupon Johns sunk back in his seat, shaking his head from side to side.

"I'm going to solve these murders and toss Knells by his belt loops out of my constabulary. You're a good man, Sergeant. Don't worry about the forced statement. Let's get to Warwickshire and help Martha and Helen. I'd better call Cousins. He'll be worried about his fiancé."

After trying to explain to Piers that it was better to let the authorities handle the situation, Johns finally threatened him with impeding an investigation if he showed up. Finally, and in record time, they pulled up at the gates of Greenwoods. There sitting in his own car was Bennie. All three men got out of their cars.

"So, the local gossip says that Lord Percy, who's about eighty, hasn't been seen in over six months. That's not unusual. He's known for being a recluse. His nephew arrived about that time and hired two women to work for him, one as a cook and the other as a general maid. Both women are not local. What do you need from me?"

"I received a call from a woman, Martha Littleword, who I believe is under threat. In the last three days, two homicides and one assault, resulting in a victim being taken to the hospital have taken place within close proximity of Mrs. Littleword. She's also a personal friend of mine and, if you would, I'd like your help."

"Let's go," Bennie replied, without hesitation.

All three men got into Johns' vehicle and turned the car into the lane. As a light snow fell, the world became deceptively quiet, holding its breath and waiting for the inevitable.

Scene Break

Tucked into the corner of the limekiln shed, Martha found a sturdy rope. Their plan was to surprise Brickstone when he came to fricassee them and tie him up, then pop him back into the kiln for safe keeping and go to the house to call Johns and Piers.

"So, here's what we'll do. Brickstone has to come through here to access the wood furnace. If he comes through the door, we'll be standing on either side and trip him with the rope. Your job, Martha, is to get the gun, if he has one, while I quickly tie his feet. What do you think?" Helen asked, her face still covered with soot and her hair completely disheveled, making her look like a deranged wilderness woman.

Martha, scrunching up her mouth, said sarcastically, "I like it. It's a good plan. The trick, for me, is not to get shot two or three times while he's floundering around on the ground."

"You sound critical," Helen replied, her tone indignant.

"Well, I've got to wrestle a loaded gun from a maniac. That's a trifle more complicated than tying flailing legs."

Helen stood back, exasperatedly. "Really? Is this a time to quibble over who does what? If you want to tie his legs, while I grab the gun, fine!"

Martha again pursed her lips. She actually liked the plan but didn't want to take chances wrangling firearms from a man.

"What if when he comes into the shed, we hit him over the head with something? That way he's easier to tie up and less likely to shoot us," Martha offered.

Helen nodded, obviously, ruminating over the adjusted plan.

"Sounds good. I don't want to kill him, though. Promise to tap him only hard enough to knock him silly. Okay?"

Martha, with her hands firmly positioned on her hips in a posture of consideration, agreed. "Let's find a rock or brick, something to whack him with."

"No. Let's try a long board. That gives us extra length. Don't want to get too close," Helen said.

"Oh, now it's about staying safely out of arms range," Martha snipped.

"Okay, what's wrong with you? You're being very touchy. Why the mood?"

Martha shuffled around the dark shed looking for a usable piece of wood to knock Brickstone out with and toeing things that might have mice or bugs under them.

"I'm sorry. I woke up in there," she gestured toward the kiln where they'd been locked up, "and the whole reality of the last few days came flooding in on me. People are dead because of me, because of some ridiculous moment in time when that crazy, nut job and I crossed paths. I didn't like Saundra and Mrs. Cuttlebirt was a gossip, but that doesn't mean they deserved what happened to them. It doesn't make sense and sometimes I need it to. Do you know what I mean?"

Martha picked up a nice sized piece of firewood and holding it with one hand, hit it a few times against her palm.

Helen stopped her own search. "Come here," she said gently.

Martha, with tears in her eyes, choked up. Salty drops pooled and wound their way down her cheeks. Still holding onto the log of wood, she went over to Helen, who wrapped her in her arms and hugged her for a long time.

"It's going to be okay. You've been through a rough patch, and there aren't answers for why bad things happen to people. Keep your faith in goodness. Believe in it, even when it's too dark to see the other side."

Through snuffles and some soft crying, Martha finally choked out, "You're one of the few people, Helen, I'd want to have in my bomb shelter. I love you. Thank you."

Helen patted Martha on her back as they both heard the footfalls coming toward the path. With looks of sheer terror, they jumped to either side of the door, Helen, with the rope and Martha, with the kindling whacker. Martha put her finger over her lips in a gesture of quiet. Helen gave her back a 'duh' expression, and they both readied themselves for the strike.

The wooden shed door swung open, allowing for more of the moonlight to penetrate the interior. A man's shadow cast itself across the dirt floor. His tread solid, he walked inside.

Martha, her heart pounding, swung for the back of his head, knocking him forward. He fell to the floor groaning and rolled over.

"What the Hell?" Brickstone mumbled.

Something snapped inside Martha and taking her foot, she gave him a firm push, rolling him back over onto his face. She jumped on his back, and grabbing his hair, she ground his face into the dirt of the shed.

"You worthless piece of human trash! How could you? How could you hurt poor defenseless, innocent people so you could have what you want! I'm going to pull every piece of your nasty, creepy hair out of your head!"

Brickstone cried and flailed under Martha's attack. Helen tied his feet and then stood back watching Martha take out all of her obvious pent up anger upon the back of Brickstone's head. It was somewhere in between a third ear pulling and a fifth thwacking between the shoulder blades that Johns, Bennie, and Endicott stepped through the door. Their flashlights danced around the dark room, landing upon Martha's red mane, whipped into a wild, unkempt storm as she pulled on a pleading Brickstone's hair.

The three policemen and Helen exchanged expressions of surprise and consternation at the spectacle happening on the floor in front of them.

Johns stepped forward and put both his hands, firmly on her shoulders. She became quiet and completely disengaged from assaulting Brickstone.

"Martha?" Johns said softly. "Please, sweetheart, get off the criminal. I'll take it from here." He lifted her up and she turned around abruptly burrowing into his chest. He held her. Endicott and Bennie picked Brickstone up off the floor, his face covered with dirt and sprigs of his hair spiking out in multiple directions.

"She's crazy!" he cried with wild-eyed fear upon his muddy face.

Martha tried to get free from Johns' embrace, probably to go after Brickstone again, but Johns held her tightly, saying, "Better be glad I don't turn her loose. She'd most likely enjoy finishing the job."

Endicott and Bennie jerked Brickstone out of the shed, leaving Johns to help Martha and Helen find their way back into the main house.

Later, the girls sat quietly in Greenwoods' library. They'd built a nice fire in the massive stone fireplace, and Helen had called Piers to explain that she was safe. With Martha's assistance, Helen was going through the various documents, manuscripts, account books and acquisition logs trying to determine what the collection had held and what had been sold. The job would take some time.

"Brickstone was thorough, to be sure, but he'd, thankfully, started with the less valuable things. He probably didn't want to attract too much attention, too fast," Helen said. She picked up a cup of steaming tea and sipped it.

Martha was studying a full-length portrait of a lovely woman dressed in a silk gown of the type fashionable during the late eighteenth century. The woman's face showed a refined grace coupled with bright, intelligent eyes.

"You know what, Helen? I think if she walked into the room at this moment, we'd like her."

"Who?" Helen mumbled, focusing only on the work before her.

"The woman in the portrait."

Helen looked up and turned her head to see who Martha was talking about. "Oh, yeah, I guess we would. She has a kind face."

"Do you see the bow and arrow she's holding in her hands? That seems unusual for a woman of that time," Martha mused.

"Actually, it was fashionable for genteel women to learn archery." Helen went back to pouring over her accounts, but added, "Gave them an outlet. Their lives were pretty constrained for the most part."

Martha continued to consider the woman in the painting. "I bet she was a force to be reckoned with. You can see her spirit in her eyes."

Johns and Sergeant Endicott walked into the room. Both women turned toward them.

"Did Brickstone tell you everything he told us?" Martha asked.

"Yes, he's on his way into Stratford's Constabulary. He's got lots of time ahead of him to think about his crimes. Lord Percy's body was collected and his nephew is being contacted. They've picked up Melissa Sutherland. She was halfway to Bath. Melissa is willing to talk."

"Well, she did save Martha and me," Helen interjected.

"Yes, that will be taken into consideration. Brickstone, on the other hand, has a lot to answer for," Johns chuckled. "But, I think the best punishment he's ever likely to receive was the thrashing you gave him, dear."

Martha gave him a loving smile and turned to Helen.

"Come on, Helen. Let's get home. I've got a child to pick up Wednesday and a house to get tidy. We can dig in this mausoleum another day."

Helen shut her books and walked over to the group ready to leave.

"Help me snuff the fire. We don't want anything to happen to this house. It's a wonder of English history. I'm going to have a friend of mine from the National Trust come down and see what he thinks they might be able to do. If the new heir wants to sell the Shakespearian documents, he'll have more than enough money to put the house and estate back to rights."

Both women unconsciously looked up at the woman's portrait over the fireplace.

"I think she'd like that," Martha said softly.

"Yes, let's do our best to make it happen," Helen added.

Johns went over and tamped out the fire. The four people left the room and made their way out to the parked vehicle. As the car pulled out of the pebbled courtyard, Martha turned back for one last look. What she saw made her nudge Helen.

"Do you see what I see?" she asked.

There in the library's long window stood a woman dressed like the one in the portrait. She raised her hand in an acknowledgment, on her face an expression of gratitude and then she was gone.

Helen and Martha exchanged smiles. The past and the present were finally reconciled.

CHAPTER 36

"One feast, one house, one mutual happiness."

-Shakespeare, Two Gentlemen of Verona, Act V, Scene IV

Practically every window at Healy was illuminated. Christmas Eve was in full swing and Piers pulled out all the stops to make it one of the most memorable the old Elizabethan pile had seen in a long time. The dining room was dressed with crisp white table linens. Beautiful hand-painted china and delicate crystal stemware graced the impressively long table. A centerpiece of candles and grape vines intertwined into the shape of a Christmas tree, festooned with evergreens and holly berries charmed everyone who saw it.

The guests arrived through the main hall and collected together in front of the massive fireplace where a log of enormous girth snapped and crackled within its stone embrace.

"Here's more mulled wine," Señor Agosto declared as he brought in a tray of clear cups full of the spicy, warm traditional drink.

All those dearest to Helen and Piers were assembled. Emerson and Christine's young son, Robert, both played with

Amos. They kept up a merry chase running up and down the long hallway, tossing toys for Amos to fetch. Martha, Kate and the new boyfriend, James, sat comfortably together on the Knole sofa and wingback chairs telling stories to Christine and her husband, Joseph about the Pudding and Pie Contest. Johns and Polly had just arrived.

Martha got up and brought them over to meet Kate and James. Polly gave Kate a warm hug and asked if she had the same fiery personality as her mother, while surreptitiously giving James, the boyfriend, a critical eye.

"Oh, most definitely, I have my Mother's no-nonsense attitude. That's what I love about her." Kate gave her mom a squeeze.

"I hear you have your constabulary back," Martha said to Johns, handing him a glass of wine.

"Yes, Knells is back at Leeds. I'm reinstated. Solving two murders and catching Brickstone put Knells in his place. It was a joy to see him off."

"Everyone, if I may have your attention, please. I'd like to make a toast," Piers said happily, gesturing for his guests to come in closer.

Once everyone was holding a glass and standing together near the fireplace, Piers raised his glass.

"I want to thank each and every one of you for sharing your Christmas Eve with us. Helen and I want you to know what you mean to us and that as long as this is our home, there's always a warm welcome for all of you."

Turning to Helen, he said gently, "Helen, I love you. Thank you for making me the happiest man alive by agreeing to marry me. I've learned the value of love, friendship and family from you, so with that in mind, I'd like to give you something special for Christmas."

Piers' eyes lifted and he nodded his head at Señor Agosto, who stood resolutely at the tall, sliding doors of the dining room. With Piers' signal, Agosto pulled back the doors and out came the remainder of Helen's children, Peter and Timothy, and their families. Helen was completely overwhelmed with joy. They descended on her with words of greeting, hugs, and loving kisses. Tears of happiness appeared on many faces, both young and old.

As family and friends were introduced, people found topics in common, laughed, talked and nibbled on Christmas treats. Helen and Martha sat together, surrounded by those they loved best and later, if things went well, they'd enjoy a fun game of hide and seek.

Wishing all of you a very merry Christmas! May your new year be blessed! Thank you for reading.

Please check out my other books in the Marsden-Lacey series:

Two Birds With One Stone

Murder Travels in Threes

Death Drinks Darjeeling

And my Willow Valley Series:

The Ghost in Mr. Pepper's Bed

Thank you!

Made in the USA
Monee, IL
26 October 2020